E.A. Maynard

AfterMath

A collection of Short Thriller Stories

———

E. A. Maynard

E.A. Maynard

AfterMath

For information contact:
E.A. Maynard
info@eamaynard.com
http://www.eamaynard.com
Book and cover design by E. A. Maynard
ISBN- 978-1-7343265-5-0

E.A. Maynard

Dedication

In my years, I had many friends that has come and gone. Some of them meant a lot to me and some were only around for a short time. This book is dedicated to my friends. They are the reason I asked the question "what happens after the story".

Telling the stories in this book is a reminder that the end of a story is only the beginning of another story that provides hope. It reminds me that even the hard times in life will pass.

Those who I have called friends have all gone on to make their own stories just as I have. I hope and pray they have the best life they can have. No matter where they are, I hope someday we can meet again, even if it is to tell our stories to each other.

To my friends, you helped me live the story of my life (and some of my writing,) and I would not change a thing. Thank you for all the time you shared with me.

E.A. Maynard

Table of Contents

E.A. Maynard

Preface

There are always lives and stories to tell after one story ends. What you will hear here are the stories of those lives changed in ways they didn't expect. For these people, everything changed when a sunny day in Risingsun, Ohio became a day of mourning for so many. This is a collection of stories that follow the book Country Secrets.

Jon Riggs starts us off with his story looking for answers. Not every answer is what you expect. Jon set out to see if he could return home again. What will he learn about the past he left behind? What will he do when he finds all the truths?

After Jon's story, we hear from Mick. Mick did not leave town like Jon and so many others. Mick stayed and continued roaming around the old towns he knew so well. The problem with staying in your hometown is that your past is never far from you.

With his past so close to home, Mick will face his past that is trying to grab and drag him back into a life he was leaving behind. There are many choices for Mick to make and each choice will lead him down different roads. Find out if Mick will rebuild the drug empire Scott Bearman left or will he leave the empire to its ruins?

Time has passed for everyone in these Stories, but for Adam (Duke) Byrd, time has passed enough that his oldest son had graduated with his master's degree. Adam is found in the back of a church by his oldest son.

In the wisdom Adam had gained through his life, he decided to share a story of his past with Scott Bearman. Adam shares a story of hardships, fear, and thrilling turns.

Even with such important members of Country Secrets, for Scott Bearman, one of the most important was Rose. Rose took the loss of Scott Bearman harder than others. She took her rage towards the person she felt was responsible for everything and became a lawyer.

Rose, as a lawyer, worked to take down any criminal she could find. She had a good life till she got the chance to take down the one person she wanted to take down the most. The problem with going after a king is that the king will come after you, too.

Next, Mark Himlee has a surprise from his past come find him. Mark didn't tell many people where he went and the visitor from his past was someone, he never thought that he would see again.

Once Mark meets with his long lost friend, there were no more secrets. Some truths are revealed and like good friends do, they told one another what had been happening.

Mark, unlike his friend, had left their hometowns to find a life of doing good things for others. Mark had even became a local hero. This is the story of how Mark's life found everything he needed.

Join Mark as he tells his tale. What Mark confesses to his friend is an example of how even good men need to do bad things for the greater good.

As exciting as the stories are that you'll hear from Jon, Mick, Adam, Rose, and Mark, Scott Bearman who is now known as Thomas Norris, gives you an adventure that is worth following. Thomas shares an adventure of his new life as a fixer. Go with him as he talks about his first solo job down in Raleigh.

E.A. Maynard

What should have been a simple job becomes filled with betrayal, surprises, and the birth of the Revenant.

Finally, we are given a look at the man who took a chance that led Scott Bearman into a world of other people's problems. This man is seen as being as hard as his name suggests.

Mr. Stone took Scott Bearman off into a world unknown to most and taught him everything he knew. Now he sees his end coming and while sitting in a hidden away bar located in Baltimore, he lets his drinks get the best of him and he tells a stranger a tale.

A tale of no good choices, but it is that tale that was the beginning of his ending. Charles Stone is not someone that is friendly to a stranger or allows others to know anything about himself.

This stranger just happened to there when Mr. Stone wanted to confess the one sin to him. As most men do, he wanted to let go of what held him for so many years. Maybe he believed you can't go to heaven with that kind of weight holding you down.

Chapter One

No Road Home

Years had passed since the day Jon Rigg had told his friends goodbye, then left for the Marines. What was once a skinny hundred-and sixty-pound brown haired teenager, he now stood on his mother's street at just under a two-hundred-pound man full of defined muscles.

It has been almost a decade since he left and has not talked to anyone since he left. His high school sweetheart broke up with him in a dear john letter. Then when he asked his family about his friends, the subject was changed. Now that he had come back to his hometown, he could find his old friends and catch up with them.

First, he had to go to his mom's house and see her for the first time in two years. Jon took the steps he needed and walked up on the porch. He couldn't help but think how different it felt to be home.

He didn't walk in because it was no longer where he lived. The porch was the same porch he sat on with a girl named Becky and this was where they both shared their first kiss. The doorbell still had the same obnoxious tone that would make him jump up when his favorite pizza was being delivered. In fact, nothing really had changed. Even the new coat of paint looked the same as the old paint.

This was his home, but it was not his house. The last time he had seen his family was for a week at a midpoint between Northwest Ohio and his short stay at the Marine base in Beaufort, SC. Before this day, he had not thought about coming back. He really felt as if he came back, he would get stuck like so many he knew.

Now that he was back, he wanted to find Dan and see how he was doing. Maybe see if Scott and Rose had had a bunch of kids. There was also Duke and Jenny, who seemed as if they were going down the road to get married, too. Jon thought about all the possibilities and what had changed in those years.

The door opened followed with a high pitched scream. His mother was hugging him and kissing his cheek. His sister and brother came out to join in welcoming him home. Other family members would be coming over later, but his siblings came over to be the first to welcome Jon home. Without a question, that is exactly what they did. His family had a bond, and they would hold that bond till the end of their days.

Before Jon realized it, he had been back for eight days. In that time, Jon expected his old friends would have heard he was back. It was not like much happens in a small town without everyone knowing. He remembered hearing about people coming back from the military that he didn't know, and that was before technology made it so easy to spread the word.

Finally, tired of waiting for his friends to come to him, he decided he would go find Dan first. He was his closest friend before leaving and figured he would be the first to come see him. In any small town, the first place to go to find someone would be their parents' house.

Jon had driven to Dan's house so many times, that he could almost drive there with his eyes closed. Except this time, when he pulled into the house he knew, it looked and felt different. It had been painted a different color and there wasn't any landscaping.

Dan's mom always made sure there was flowers and the property looked welcoming.

Now the greyish blue house had stones wrapping around it. All the flower beds had been removed and nothing remained other than Jon's memories. For some reason, Jon knew that he would not get his answers by knocking on the door. None the less, he still made the attempt.

With three quick knocks, he stepped back and waited. It was not even thirty seconds when a guy that looked to be in his mid-forties answered. A well-built man but he had most likely not worked out for some time. With a demanding voice, he asked what he could do to help.

Jon asked about his friend Dan and Dan's family. All the guy could tell Jon was how he got a great deal on the house five years before. From what he heard, the couple was going through a divorce, and neither of them wanted the house. Jon thanked him and left.

Instead of going home, Jon went to a local bar in Fostoria. It was a place on route one 99 and from what he remembered, it used to be a popular spot. Since it was late in the afternoon and the party crowd wouldn't be out yet, he wanted to see the place and get a beer. Pulling up to the red building, he found a few cars parked in the lot. Looking around, he would have guessed about six cars were there.

Walking in, he saw an old guy at the bar, a couple at a table holding hands, and a group of guys who seemed to have started drinking way too early. Jon had no interest in dealing with any of them. He sat down at the bar taking plenty of space for himself, so no one Would sit next to him. "What do you want to drink? Just know my mix drinks suck, but I make a mean whiskey on the rocks." The bartender told him.

"I am not much of a whiskey guy, but I will take a corona. Thanks", the bartender gave Jon a serious look before turning around to get the corona as he asked. When he returned, he put down the beer and a shot of vodka. Then said "You remind me of a guy I knew who liked his vodka. So, this one is on me."

Jon didn't respond and the bartender went back to prepping for the late-night crowd. It was not long when one of the drunken guys came up to him trying to make small talk. The guy smelled horrible and could not get more than three words out without slurring.

Jon made small talk and the drunken man offered Jon to join him and his friends. Before he was able to answer, the drunk guy yelled at the bartender telling him he wanted another round and it was on his new friend.

Jon knew this old trick and was in no mood to play. The bartender must have noticed the look on Jon's face and told the guy that he was cutting them off. With the logic you find from a drunk person, he started to yell at Jon about doing something to get him cut off.

It was annoying and this was not what Jon wanted. Hell, he just wanted to have a beer, then maybe see if he could find his friends Scott or Duke. Finally, Jon had enough, put a ten on the counter and went to leave. When he turned to go out the door, the drunk guy grabbed his shoulder.

It should be understood that Jon had two things going in his favor. He had been in enough bar fights that he knew what was happening and was ready. The other thing was, he had been trained by the US government to defend himself and country.

When Jon turned back, he already had a hold on the guy's wrist. He twisted the guy's wrist and turning his arm, pushed the drunk down and planted his face on the bar. Jon told the guy he needs to relax and let him leave, and three of the other drunk guys joined their buddy and tackled him to the ground.

One guy kept punching the ground, while another guy punched his friend's back, and the third guy was punching Jon and the floor. It looked to be something out of a Three Stooges' film. The only difference was Larry, Curly, or Mo were not there. Instead, he had three drunks laying on him. That was until the bartender came around and pulled the guys off of him.

As Jon began to get up, he noticed the first guy had his hands cuffed behind his back. The other guys laid on the floor with their hands on the back of their head. Looking up, the bartender was holding a pistol. Considering Jon was unarmed and still at a position that put him at a disadvantage, he put up his hands and went to lay down like the other guys.

Before he did, he heard "Riggs, get your ass up. I know you didn't start this." Hearing his old nickname, Jon was taken back. He just could not place how the bartender knew him. He went to ask who he was, but a few cops came in the front door. As if this was not their first time, they walked up and picked up the four guys. While the guys were being dragged out, one cop stop and talked to the bartender.

They talked for a while and were joking around. Who is this guy, Jon wondered? At least that was what Jon was asking himself. One of the cops came over to him and began to talk about the guys having a habit of causing fights. As the officer was wrapping up, he told Jon "I hear you're a Marine. I won't hold that against you. I was in the Navy. Don't worry, your name will not be mentioned in the report. Take care of yourself."

With that, he was gone, the bartender was back behind the bar as though nothing happened, and a few of the late night crowd started to come in. Jon went to leave again, but saw he was being waved over by the mysterious bartender.

All Jon could think about was how he just wanted to get out of the bar. Now the bartender wanted to talk to him. Considering the bartender could have let him get taken away with the other drunks, he felt he should at least thank him.

As he got back to the old wooden bar, he heard "Riggs, right? That is what you use to go by if I remember correctly." And that was not at all what he expected. He could only answer with a yes and a questioning stare.

The bartender reached out his hand and finally laid it all out. "I am Mick. I don't know if you remember me. It has been a while and we were not close. You spent your time with that Dan guy, Duke and my business partner Scott. I figured since you were friends with Scott, I owed him to help you. And really that is all I wanted to say. If you ever want to come in for a drink and some talk, I am here most nights and days."

As Mick walked away, Jon yelled for him. "I have some questions, like where is everyone? My family won't tell me anything about anyone."

Mick began to look down towards the floor as if he didn't want to share what he knew. Then said "Come back tomorrow around one. This is not the time; we can talk tomorrow when no one else here. I can answer everything for you then."

Jon went to say something but stopped himself. Realizing that the bar was filling up and it would be hard for Mick to talk, he left. While going back to his mom's house, he decided to change his plans and started heading towards his brother's house outside of Risingsun.

When Jon pulled into the driveway, Frank came out. It was like he was waiting for him. Whether he was or not, Jon wanted to push for answers. He would be talking to Mick, but he needed to start getting answers. If he wanted to find out what happened, he needed to start hearing some of the stories.

When Jon got out of his car, his brother just stood on the porch holding a brown bottle of beer. They didn't say a word to each other until Jon got on the porch, when he noticed an old cooler. The blue cooler was nothing impressive and looked as it should have been thrown out years ago. There was even a small stream of water coming from the bottom corner.

"So, do you plan to share or did you forget how to offer a guest something to drink?" Jon's comment got Frank to laugh. Reaching down into the cooler, Frank asked "Are you able to handle another drink? You look like you already had a rough time and it smells like you've had a beer or two already. I thought you Marines were an unstoppable force."

After that, they sat on the porch watching cars go by and traded insults till Jon felt that his brother was relaxed enough and said "What happened when I left? Why is no one telling me about my friends?"

"You know mom pushed you to go to the military because your friends had a bad reputation. Hell, if I remember right, one of them was running his own small crime family. When you left, we only heard rumors and not very often. I heard one of your friends was killed and another ran off." Jon stopped his brother before he could go on.

"What do you mean killed? One of my friends was killed?" Jon looked to be in shock and as his brother tried to answer him, Jon put up his hand. He could not believe that it could happen to one of his friends. He started to remember what they had gotten themselves into.

Jon looked back to his brother and nodded his head. With that, Frank went on. "I don't remember who did what. It has been so many years ago, it feels like an urban legend now. I can tell you that there is still one person who you hung out with back then who is still around. It's that girl you were dating before you left. I saw her in Fostoria a month ago at Kroger's.

She recognized me and we talked a bit. From what she says, she is married to some guy that she had a kid with. She appeared to be happy. So, I would suggest you not bother her. There is nothing good to come from trying to bring up the past with a married woman. I would not take it too calmly if my wife's ex tried to come back into her life. You know what I mean?"

Jon nodded his head to his brother. He knew that it would only cause problems for her. There was no reason to do that to her. She was a good girl back in his day and she would have never done something like that to him.

Jon asked "Do you know a guy named Mick? He works down at the bar on Route one 99."

Frank told Jon "I have heard of him. I also heard that place has a questionable reputation. I don't know if its rumors or something more. Some of my friends joke about that being the place to get drugs. All you have to do is put a twenty on the table."

There was nothing left of the topic to discuss, so they discussed the last eight years that he had been gone. Before either of them realized it, they were both drunk and passed out on the living room floor.

With a heavy pounding head, the brothers were woke up by Frank's wife. Like the good wife she was, she gave them both a kick and told them to get off the floor. "You two look like a pair of worthless dogs. Get up and clean yourselves up."

As she walked away, there was some more things said, but nothing nice. Jon heard everything, but only told his sister-in-law good morning. Frank on the other hand asked his wife is she wanted sex or food.

All three of them laughed when she stuck her head out of the bedroom and told Frank to make some coffee and pancakes.

It was a good start to the day while the three of them talked and ate their breakfast. The brothers for the most part felt like they were back to normal, and Frank's loving wife went to bed.

This time, the brothers sat on the porch with a cup of coffee. Frank gave a warning to Jon, "Don't dig up the past. It was not as nice as you'd like to remember. A lot of people got hurt and some might hold a grudge against your friends."

Jon remembered the parties, the girls, and the hell they all raised. Then again, there were fights, drugs, and other troubles that came to mind. That is what got him wondering if his childhood was much different than others. Were he and his friends really as bad as it seemed that his brother was making them out to be?

With nothing left to be said, Jon drove back to Fostoria. He parked his car at an old ice cream shop and walked around. He had nowhere to go and no one to see till noon. He needed to figure out what it was he needed to know.

What struck him was how his hometown was no longer his town. Walking in his hometown, people could stop to talk to him if he was walking. He would see people he knew and feel at ease. What he thought would be a pleasant walk, ended by him seeing familiar faces that in reality either turned away, or gave him the impression that they wanted to do something evil to him.

This was not his home, but a place he would come back to see his family. Jon finally realized that his home was somewhere out there, but he just needed closure here to go find it. Only then could Jon leave to have the life he wanted.

Finally, he walked into the bar. There sat Mick with papers covering a table and a cup of coffee next to him. It felt odd to Jon to see a bar with all the lights on. The filth and grime, the walls looking so plain, and just an empty feeling filled the place. Seeing the bar for what it was, he wondered how he or others found these places so alluring.

Mick looked up from his papers and waved Jon over. "Riggs, how are you? I am glad you came back. Have a seat and I will get you a drink." Mick started talking again when he got behind the bar.

"How would you like my special drink? I promise it will make you feel great."

Jon went to answer when he noticed Mick playing with an espresso machine. Mick didn't wait for an answer and was halfway through when Jon sat down at Mick's table. "What are you doing here? It looks like you're doing the bar's books."

Mick told him that is what owners do. Then said "I can tell you my story later. You didn't come here to talk about me. You want to know what happened to everyone you knew. So, let me start with a few happy stories that happened here."

The look on Jon's face told him to start telling everything.

"Ok, so let me start with Duke. I think it was around the time you left. He and Bearman had started to plan on how both of them could get out of everything. Duke had gotten engaged to his girlfriend. Even with all the craziness that happened, he found a way to escape the madness.

After everything crashed and the world seemed to have ended for a lot of us, Duke and I went to Bearman's lawyer. Fortunately, Bearman had the foresight to set up a plan for us to protect ourselves from a big bust.

Lots of cops, public people, and powerful people went down. Duke had a book with everything Bearman knew. All his contacts and their details were in that book. Not many people got out without paying heavily.

Duke and his girl went down to Columbus where he became a preacher. From what I have heard, he is good at it too." Mick stopped for a moment to think about the past.

Then Mick's face became very sour. It looked as though he was close to becoming emotional and needed time to think before continuing. Instead of saying anything immediately, he got up and went to get himself a coffee.

Neither of them said a thing while Mick got his coffee and returned. As he slid the chair back under himself and sat down, he got a little smile.

"You know that Scott Bearman was a hell of a guy. With all of his flaws, he would go to the end of the earth to help a friend. If someone tried to cross me, Bearman would be there and put them in their place.

He was a real friend to all of us. Those of us who worked for him had never known anyone so good to us. I had the chance once to save him and show him that I was there for him. That was one of my proudest days.

You see, things changed quickly. Jay Himlee was buried, then Mark Himlee left town. Bearman told me he gave Mark money to go do something different and get out of this life. Since his brother was dead, Mark didn't feel like he had to stay.

When the Himlee brothers were out of the picture, we grew and spread out. We had business going in Toledo and more towns.

Then after a gun deal went south, we made an enemy of a group out of Detroit. I still think they are the ones who killed Bearman."

Jon spoke up. "Wait a minute, Bearman is dead? You're telling me that Jay died, but not how. Then you tell me Bearman was killed by a group from Michigan. What the hell happened?"

Mick gave it some thought on how to answer Jon. "According to the papers, Jay killed a girl and hung himself outside of Fostoria. The found a knife with blood all over it, and blood all over his hands. As far as I am concerned, Jay got off easy. Either way, Jay was done causing problems and our lives got better.

Bearman on the other hand, went to a little area that not many people knew about in Risingsun to make a deal. He told me it was his last deal and if I remember correctly, he wrote a note to Rose saying the same thing.

He also told Duke that the raid was coming in a day or so after that deal, and that is why we went to Bearman's lawyer. It was what Bearman told us to do.

Well, I heard about Bearman while I was sitting at a table with Duke across from some lady making a deal for our immunity. She told us that Bearman was found dead in a burned-out truck. There was no expression or sympathy from her or her people. That lady was colder than anyone I had ever met.

I don't know how Duke kept himself together, but I fell apart. Once I pulled myself together, we finished the agreement. I got to keep everything I had and so did Duke. We turned over all the information we had and there was a lot of arrest made.

Dan was missing and people assumed that he had something to do with Bearman's death. The rumor that many people repeated was that Dan found some drug rivals to Bearman, then had them help kill him.

I heard his parents split a few years after that. As for Duke, he left town with that Jenny girl and they never came back. Rose left for college and got married to a guy she met down there. I used to check in on her, but once she got married, I stopped hearing from her. Some of the guys that used to work under Bearman used to stop in here to talk, but that came to an end too.

Now no one from our old life is around. That is why I am excited to see you. I don't expect you to be around long, but an old face is nice."

Mick stopped talking and seemed to get a half smile, as a thought from the past came back to him and it was a good memory. He looked at Jon shortly after that and apologized.

"No need to apologize, it sounds like life went to hell after I left. Was Dan ever found?" Jon asked.

Jon noticed Mick didn't have anything to say, so he decided to fill Mick in on his life and what had happened to him.

"You know, after I got out of boot camp, I got stationed at a few places. I was in Cuba, then Japan, and once I started to think I was going to sail through the marines, I found I had a dangerous assignment.

E.A. Maynard

I can't go into details, but I found myself in the Middle East. We went to secure an American property. I had to go with a team of six to hold at the rear entrance. While we were there, the mission went to hell.

A man came running up towards us. We all pulled up our guns. I don't know if it was me or one of the other guys, but he was shot in the chest. That stopped him, but a bomb strapped to him went off.

That is when the others came rushing towards us. There was not much time, so I told the team to get in and close the gate. The banging and the shouting were so loud! It was like nothing I had heard before.

We knew that the people on the other side wanted us dead. When we were told to get up front with the rest of the squad, we double timed it. It was a good thing too.

Once the last of my team got into the building, you could hear the back gate start to give way. None of us looked back, until a loud explosion came from behind. Then we heard the cheering of the mob. I think we all knew they had gotten through.

It felt like a mile sprint to get up front with the everyone else. I started to feel safe, as if we got away. Then Quincy got shot and dropped to the ground.

Only my leed and I saw Quincy fall. The other guys kept running while we stopped to pick up our brother.

As we got down to pick him up, it was a shooting range. Everyone with a gun could and did fire it. There was no time to think, only act. I guess that is what all that training was for. Because I just reacted and pulled Quincy to the truck.

He was screaming and asking us to save him. I would have pissed myself if I could, that's how scared I was. The bullets were going both ways and more of them were coming to close to me.

Once we got close enough, two of the guys in the truck grabbed Quincy and pulled him in. We got in as quickly as we could behind him. Our driver didn't wait for any commands and took off. The dirt flew and the gun fire didn't sound as scary the farther away we got.

After that, Quincy was sent home with an honorable discharge. I heard he couldn't get past what all happened. I was given metals and was the talk of the base. That was all good till I got transferred. Since then, I have risked my life to save my brothers.

Jon had to stop, not for any other reason than it was too hard on him. Jon had lived a life of adventure and those who live adventures tend to carry a lot of pain. The thing was the emotional pain was written all over his face.

Mick was able to read it and changed the topic. "After the life you lead, coming back here must have taken a lot. If I got out when I was younger, I don't think I would have come back. On top of that, you now know what happened or at least the overview. This leaves me with one question. What are you going to do now?"

The question was one Jon had been asking himself since he came back to Ohio. Jon knew a choice had to be made. As he was being asked the question, he knew his answer without a doubt.

"Mick, thank you. You have helped me more than you know. I was on the fence, but I know I need to go home." Jon got up and started walking out.

"Hey, are you going back to your mom's? Mick shouted.

"No, I am going back to the Marines. I have family there and they need me more than this place does. Plus, I don't see myself fitting in here with all the things I have been through. I am going back to the only place I had ever felt was my home." Jon gave a smile and walked out.

Aftermath (Bearman Series)

Since then, Jon has not been seen in Ohio again. He went back to his life of adventures and proudly kept bearing the pain so others could live to see another day.

E.A. Maynard

Chapter Two

Bar Fly

There have been a few rough years since I heard what happened to Bearman. I remember all the good times and I still try to keep a little of what he built alive.

After Bearman was killed, many who worked for us left. They didn't want to be involved in a life that could lead to the same end as they heard happened to the great Scott Bearman.

I have to admit, it was horrible to hear, and I don't blame those who went their own way. To be honest, I should have done the same. I had a good start with a house of my own and enough money I could have lived off of for at least three years.

But that is not what I did.

I had it in my head that I owed my friend.

Now looking back, I realized that I didn't keep selling drugs because of Bearman. I did it because I had been taking over the business. I needed to prove that I could run the business and Scott Bearman would not have been as big without me.

What I didn't realize till a few years later was that people still feared me because they didn't know Bearman was dead. Once the power from the Bearman name was gone, I found myself back to pushing drugs on the streets.

The money was not great, and I finally broke down. I still had some money, but I knew at this rate, my house would not be able to be kept up for much longer.

The only other option I had was to find a real job. The problem was my skill set didn't match too many jobs.

It was not till a week after deciding to get a job that I found one. It was the strangest thing I had ever heard that happened. At least strange in the world I lived in.

I sat down at this bar right outside of a small town called Fostoria, Ohio. I stopped in for a beer before going home. Really, I just wanted to be around other people, the beer was just the cost to have the feeling I was with other people.

As I sat down and looked around, I saw there were only about eight people in the place. There was not a lot of talking, but it was more than I had at home. Then the bartender came up to me for my order. Keeping it simple, I ordered myself a bud light and I was about to lean back into my chair.

The bartender was quick with the drink and then kept talking to me. Come to find out, he was the owner of the place. He likes to try and know everyone who comes into his place.

He seemed nice to me and that was all I cared about. Plus, he was the first person I talked to in days that didn't want to buy some drugs off of me.

So, we talked for a while, and I had three beers. Finally, I had to get up and go. I didn't want to get too drunk and then drive. I had enough problems, adding a DUI was something I didn't need.

As I was paying my bill, the old guy I had been talking to asked me a question that seemed to change my life.

"I've seen people like you come in here. Most times your kind is looking for answers. So, what answers are you looking for? You might notice I have been around a while, so I might have an answer."

It seemed simple enough, but when I explained that I have a record, which made it tough to find a real job. I figured he would give me some crap like to hold on and push forward.

I have heard that from so many people already.

Instead, He looked me over and told me he wanted me to come in on Friday by four o'clock in the afternoon.

If I could make it to midnight, then I have a job.

After that Friday, I found I enjoyed being at the bar and most of the people that came in. It didn't take me long to realize that I wanted nothing to do with my old life. That is why I started to get rid of all the drugs. That was also when I quit smoking weed.

It should have been so simple. All the guys I know from the days of Scott Bearman had done it. I was the last holdout that I knew of.

I found that I like working at the bar. The first rule of the bar was no use or sales of "illegal items". This rule made it impossible for me to sell and keep my job.

I mean, almost all my deals were done at night, and I worked five nights a week at the bar. I would make a few sales, but it was nothing I would be able to live off of.

This made it easy to follow the first step. I started turning away people who were trying to buy. I would tell them I am out of the game. I no longer have any product. What I did have left, I sold to a guy I knew who thought he would be the next big thing.

I didn't spend much time with him. The guy wanted to talk about what Scott and I did. How did we build up so quickly and so on? That is part of my past that I was trying not to talk about. Unless you lived through that time with us, our world was a blur of events, and I don't think I could tell everything properly anymore.

After that, I was finally done.

I was like everyone else. I kept to myself after work and was the guy I needed to be at work. Things were good for me.

At least that is what I thought. I was three months into my new life and someone from my past pulled into my driveway.

He was an old friend that sold drugs for me. Now he works at a factory outside of Fremont and lives with a girl in a house he rented.

I was happy to see him.

He and I always had good conversations.

We chatted about the year that has passed since we had seen each other, as though nothing had ever happened. The talking went on for about an hour before I cut the conversation off.

"Kyle, it's been a year and I am glad to see you. I know you didn't stop to catch up. So, what are we beating around the bush for?"

Kyle was not sure what to say. He looked at his feet, then looked back up at me. "Mick, I might have caused you some problems. I don't know if you really have anything to worry about, but I pissed off a guy trying to talk himself up. Don't think I meant to make any issues for you.

I was buying a bag of weed off this guy.

You might know him. His name is Tommy, and he was telling everyone that he was your replacement.

I started to laugh, and he went on telling a group of people that you turned everything over to him.

Then said you were giving him advice on how to become the next Bearman.

I lost it and that is where I spoke up. I told him that he will never be the next Bearman, Mick, or any of the guys who worked for them.

I told him that I knew Bearman and was still friends with him.

Let's just cut to the quick.

I told Tommy to shut up and to remember that no one will think of him as the same level as Bearman. I mean this Tommy guy is a street dealer who thinks he is a kingpin.

Scott was a boss and never wanted anyone to know."

I stopped Kyle by raising my hand. I knew this Tommy guy. Tommy was the guy I sold my stock to. I don't know where he got his mindset that I was trying to guide him. The guy was not smart and if he did grow beyond selling a dime bag, he would get himself busted.

Normally, I would think this would be nothing to worry about, but Kyle would not come to me if this was nothing. That is why I thanked him for coming to tell me.

We talked a little while longer before he left. It was nice to see my friend. It was nice to see anyone who I didn't have to watch what I said around.

I went along with my life and heard things from people at the bar. Mostly about this Tommy guy asking around about me. It kind of made me chuckle since he was also telling people that I was training him to be the next big thing.

What got me to think I needed to protect myself was when I heard about this Tommy guy shooting a customer that made a joke about him trying to be the next Scott Bearman.

From what I heard; it went similar to this.

The customer just got a dime bag of weed from Tommy. Then the customer said, "You know, I am glad you're not a big deal, I would have to find a new dealer." Tommy got upset and asked what was meant by that and pulled out a gun.

The customer started to stammer and once he put his thoughts back together, he told Tommy that Bearman will become an urban legend around here. The more the guy talked, the more Tommy felt upset that people don't look at him like they did Bearman. You could see the anger build up on Tommy's face.

There was a story that Scott Bearman has been seen out looking for the person who killed him. It is like the mother who lost her baby in a river a hundred years ago. People still say they see her walking down rivers looking for her lost child. People love a good ghost story.

Tommy could not handle that and what appears to have been by mistake, he pulled the trigger. The gun was pointed at the customer's leg. What got me was how it was said that Tommy looked more shocked than the customer did.

After that, I started keeping my 9mm with me. I remember something being told to me. "Ambition and bullets are a dangerous thing. No matter what, someone with the same ambition will find you. My bet is they will have bullets too."

I let another few days go by before I decided I was not going to wait for Tommy. I started to get pissed off hearing about this teenager who was trying to make a name off of my back.

Aftermath (Bearman Series)

The more I thought about it, I thought about what Scott and I have done. I have been the one who got rid of Jay Himlee. I had shot men to save Bearman. I was a man not to be tested, and this "boy" thinks he will walk in to take me down.

I left the drug game and now I have to go back. I didn't want to go, but I was left with no choice. So, I didn't make a lot of noise with my plan. Instead, I called Kyle.

When we talked, I made it clear what I wanted. I told Kyle that I want Tommy to meet me in front of the Fostoria Police station.

This made Kyle laugh because he was the one who gave me the idea.

He used to get high and talk about how he finds it funny to think of criminals making deals and have meetings in front of the police. He was always talking about selling on the streets with a cop car in sight.

The concept was a simple one. If you try anything, you will have to face the police within seconds. I knew Tommy would not be smart enough to think it through and would agree, thinking he could make it work out in his favor.

What Tommy didn't know, Scott and I had cops on our payroll. Some of them came to like us, too. Two of them come into the bar every so often and I give them a free beer.

In return, they help keep the bar safe.

I would have expected Tommy to show up with some friends so he could try to make a scene. I was hoping that he would be that stupid.

Instead, he showed up by himself. We sat on a bench, and I let him start. He almost sounded like he was going to cry when he spoke, with a wimpering voice. "Why won't you teach me? I figured you would feel forced to teach me if I was telling people, you were. No one believed me and I got laughed at. Now I can't turn back. My friends have been telling everyone that I am going to teach you a lesson."

I didn't let him go on and made it clear that he was going to regret life if he kept going. I said "Tommy, let me explain a few things to you. The movies don't show real life. You saw that when you shot that guy in the leg.

Everyone thinks of themselves as the hero in their own story. There are reasons that lots of people don't have stories told about them.

Those people are the side characters. They are the obstacles that must be removed to get to the real challenge. You are not even an obstacle. If anyone tells our story, you should be happy if anyone can even remember your name.

I was once big and there are things, I did that will never be told. That is what should scare you. I have killed and I have made people suffer in ways you had never thought of."

Looking off as I was telling him this, I finally turned to look at him. When he locked his eyes onto mine, I gave him a fair warning. "If you want to be my enemy, you will find yourself facing a horror that will be far beyond what you can handle."

Then I got up to leave Tommy there. I figured he would think about what was said. That was not what he did. He stood up after I was about twelve feet away and yelled.

"I will make you regret not doing what I wanted. You will not make me look worthless. I am Tommy and once I am done, no one will talk about you or Bearman." Then in the fashion of a little kid, he stomped off huffing.

It would have been nice to think that this kid would calm down and go back to his dream of grandeur.

At least that is what I was hoping for.

For a couple days, I started to think that was what happened. That was, until I went to work and there were two guys leaning against a car in the parking lot.

Something told me that they were not there for a drink. When I closed my car door, they looked over towards me and made their way in my direction.

We met in an area with no cars and plenty of room to move around. As I prepared for the worse, one of the guys began to speak.

"Mick, you don't know us, but we know of you. You and Bearman were good people. I know of the stories of what you guys did to protect yours. So don't think I am here for my personal reasons.

My brother and I made a deal with Tommy before we knew it was you. You see, we get some crack for giving you a beat down."

This was interesting to me. I guess Tommy never understood how the mind of an addict works. The good thing for me was that I did.

So, I asked them a few questions. First, I asked if they have been paid. When they said no, I asked if they saw the crack. With them looking at each other, I could see the questions start to form in their minds.

That is why I put the final point out to them. "Let me get this right. You agreed to come here to beat me up, but you have not gotten anything more than a promise.

I bet he didn't even tell you how much crack you would get. I only say this because I didn't realize that Tommy was able to get crack.

But you have a job to do, and I have to get to work myself. I personally at least give half upfront in good faith, but I am sure a teenager would not try to make you guys look like a fool."

That is all it took to get them pissed off beyond belief. They walked quickly back to their car and whatever they were saying, it was not anything good.

Since they were gone, I continued walking into the bar. My hands were shaking since that was a close call for me. Those guys could have beaten me stupid.

When I went to enter the bar, my boss opened the door. Looking at me with a crowd already behind him, he stepped outside with me. The door closed behind him, and I knew he must have been watching the cameras.

The old man said, "Mick, I don't know what you are completely going through, but you need to get your shit straight."

My response was as honest as I could be with him. "Sir, I will get this taken care of. All I am trying to do was leave my old life behind, and someone is wanting to hold onto me."

I figured I would have been told to get to work and keep my problems away from the bar. At least that would be what I would have told an employee. What the old man said was much more powerful.

"Let me tell you something. I heard rumors of some kid trying to make a name for himself. Remember people like to talk and talk more as they get lubed up with some drinks.

There are only a few choices you have. It looked like the kid is taking action against you. So, you can either do nothing and hope that he would get the hint.

I don't think you're that type. I think you're similar to me. You know every action has a reaction. Don't think I am telling you to do anything that will get you in trouble. I am saying that I will have your back if you need it.

So, figure out what reaction will end this. Don't tell me or anyone what you'll do. Just do it, finish it, and let's get our lives back in order."

After that, he let me think for about ten seconds when he made a joke about how I need to get in the action of serving drinks so there is a reaction of cash coming in.

I did my job and was johnny on the spot. I made some good tips, too. I went on with my daily life and thought about what I could do to end Tommy from bothering me.

It was about a week and a half when I remembered a plan Bearman had made to deal with Jay Himlee.

I remembered everything was in place and all I needed to do is make sure nothing happened to what he had created.

I went out the next morning to look for the holes. As part of the plan, multiple holes were dug. These holes were about four feet by four feet wide and six feet deep. The holes were covered to keep them safe and marked with a large rock that had a smiley face drawn on it.

The first two holes I checked had collapsed in and were leaving a large dip in the ground. There were even some trees that fell down when the ground gave way.

The third hole though, that was intact. I found it back in some woods on Holcomb Road. I found it funny that this was the one I found intact. So much has happened on Holcomb Road, and so many stories kept kids out of those woods.

I could only imagine that the guys who dug this hole wanted to make sure they didn't have to come back.

When I looked in the hole, branches were lining the walls. Some water had filled the bottom of the hole, but it was perfect.

I could put Tommy in there for a few days to teach him a lesson. Let him know that I am the last person he would want to mess with.

Now I am left with finding him and getting him to Holcomb Road. I was happy that I would be able to end this. Plus, the stories that would be told would keep others from coming after me. It would be over.

You know the nice thing about a stupid drug dealer? Let me tell you. They tend to do the same thing every day. They go to the same places and they go to the same people. They don't think how easy it makes it for cops or someone they have pissed off to find them.

Tommy is a stupid dealer and likes to stay around a six-block area. That means that I just need to pick my day and sit where there is not a lot of people.

Fremont, where Tommy sells, has several places where that can be achieved. So, after a few days, I decided to take off Wednesday and go find him.

It was not that Wednesday was anything special, I just imagined most people would be more likely to be in their homes during the middle of the week.

That left me to have someone call Tommy and set up a meet. It was a simple thing to do. My guy was a crack head and all I had to do was give him a bit of money. Then give him Tommy's number along with instructions on where to have Tommy meet him.

I can picture the call.

First Tommy would answer with a "What". Of course, he would want to make himself feel like he is a tough guy.

The crack head would say "I was told you could help me with my eight–ball problem."

Tommy in turn would pick up with what is being said and tell the crack head that he could and ask where he was.

Another few exchanges would happen, then Tommy would leave his house to meet his new customer. No questions about the guy or how he got his number. This goes back to the stupid dealer's way of thinking.

This is why it was so easy to catch him. I was sitting in my maroon boat. Really, it's a Mercury Grand Marquis, but I spent a lot of time making this boat something beautiful.

The nice thing about driving a big car is the trunk. With the amount of space in there, you could hide a few people in there and have room for groceries.

So, when Tommy walked by me, I pulled out my 9mm and walked up behind him. With my gun shoved in between his shoulder blades, I calmly told him what to do. First, I warned him to not react and HE WAS to give me his gun. He understood I was not joking when I followed up the instructions by telling him he would be shot and die there on the street if he didn't obey.

Once he showed he understood, I grabbed his shoulder with my other hand and guided him to the trunk of my car. Getting him to climb in was no problem either. He was so submissive, I started to feel bad.

Then I remember the last person who came after me and my friends. I still have the scar on my stomach. I pushed my self pity down and shut the trunk. I was not going to go through that again. This kid was nothing near what the Himlee brothers were, but a crazy person can still do a lot of damage.

The forty-five-minute drive gave me time to think. I thought about what I would say if I was questioned about Tommy. I thought about how long I would leave Tommy in that hole.

Then my mind went to what would he do when I let him out.

Aftermath (Bearman Series)

What I am doing might get him to straighten up
or it might push him completely over the edge. This is
something I would have to make a decision on.

When we got to the woods on Holcomb Road, I
remember that Bearman once told me to follow the
plans we make. He said "Plans are made for a reason.
Fear is what destroys a plan."

Nothing left to do, but what I came to do. That is
what I said when I got out of my car and walked to the
trunk. As soon as I opened it, I took a few steps back. I
know I would have tried to find a way to escape if I
was in Tommy's shoes.

When he sat up, he looked like he was crying.
He then started to tell me how he would make me
regret whatever I was going to do. He was nothing
more than another kid trying to be a tough guy. The
problem is someone pretending will do things like
shoot a guy in the leg.

After he finished his tough-guy rant, I made him
get out of the trunk and we walked into the woods. I
was not sure what he thought his speech would do,
but I was not going to change a thing I planned.

Marching Tommy through the dark and creepy woods, I found the hole again. I didn't feel good about opening while Tommy looked on. I had a feeling he was planning something. The only thing I could think of was to have Tommy lay on the ground. Once he had and he put his hands on top of his head with the fingers interlaced, I got to work.

Moving the rock from the cover was a little tougher since it had a film of mist on it. My hands slipped a few times, but I got it moved and the cover off the hole. That is when I noticed Tommy trying to spew threats towards me. He must have thought that I had some fear of him.

I don't know why he would believe I did, but I would show him what it meant to fear someone. I learned fear when I faced what I thought was my death.

I pulled him up from the ground and he made more noises that sounded like he was trying to say something.

Maybe he saw the hole and realized what was about to happen. There were several maybes, but within six steps, he fell into the hole. There was no maybe about that.

First, I heard a yelp and then a splashing. I guess there was more water than I thought. While he was in shock and not sure what to make of his situation, I put the cover back on.

It was heavy enough that it took me some effort to get it back over the hole.

When the cover was in place, Tommy started to react. He pounded on the metal plate. I heard him start to curse me and change to crying. I believe when he heard me roll the large stone back onto the plate, it sunk in that this was not a joke.

I waited a few minutes before I started to talk to him. It was hard before with the loud crying. I said "Tommy, here is the deal. I am going to leave you here for three days. The plate has holes for air, and you will be fine. I will warn you not to mess with the walls."

Tommy was not making any noise and I figured he had accepted what was his fate, so I walked away proud of myself. I might have been feeling a bit cocky too and that is why I said, "Behave and I will see you soon Buttercup."

Normally three days doesn't seem like a long time. I imagined that Tommy felt different. My three days seem to have a lot of things going on.

First, I meet a girl at the bar. She was there with some friends that were drinking up a storm, but she was the designated driver. She had soda and we talked between customers. It was a great feeling and I got so excited when she asked if I was going to take her out for dinner.

I offered her lunch and we set a date. Her beautiful brown hair and her cute little self-bounced back with her friends after that.

I had her name, her number, and her address so I could pick her up.

When I thought that was the best the evening could get, after I closed down the bar, the old man pulled me aside and told me that I was now the bar manager. This means he would be cutting back coming in and I would be responsible for everything.

He joked about how he needs to start working less because his old bones were starting to get to him.

If you knew the old man like I got to, you would not have believed that. He was a machine and could probably outwork most machines. I only smiled and thanked him.

The following day, I went to free Tommy. I had a feeling that my past would stay buried, and I was going to be able to move on. So, when I walked into the Holcomb woods, I thought Tommy would have learned a lesson.

What I saw when I got about thirty feet away what the ground had a large indent. I knew that sight from when I went to the other holes. It was what happened when the holes collapsed in on themselves.

My heart dropped to my stomach. I walked faster and almost at a running pace to get there. I didn't have to move the rock or the plate this time. They had flipped off when the dirt on one side of the hole gave way.

I dug for Tommy, I dug and moved dirt for more than an hour. It looked as he got free since I could not find any sign of him. I could only guess that he risked my warning about the walls and wanted out at any cost.

My mind wondered if he would try to report me or what he would do. That is why I called Kyle and had him look into Tommy for me. I just told him that Tommy had not done anything, or I have not heard anything about him in some time.

What Kyle found out was that Tommy was found in Bowling Green walking around. All of his friends and family thought he lost his mind and checked him into the hospital. It was about four years before he got out.

When he did, he was convinced that he imagined it all. Even the fight he tried to have with me he believed was all in his head.

For me, that girl I had a date with is now my wife. We even have a little girl running around the yard playing with her younger brother.

It's a good life and my past is dead.

I had become a normal guy. I became that guy you see in the store and don't think anything about.

Aftermath (Bearman Series)

I am no longer the bar manager, but part owner. The old man comes in and we talk. He likes to talk about his old bones and my beautiful family. His arthritis had gotten to him, and he retired for the second time.

That old man one day asked me over for a glass of wine on a summer evening and asked how I took care of my problem all those years ago. I had never lied to the old man or my wife. So, I told him the whole story. What surprised me was how proud he seemed that I didn't back down.

To this day, the old man is the only one who knows. Now I guess you do too.

E.A. Maynard

Chapter Three

The Father's Sins

An old grey-haired pastor sat in a church praying, which was not unusual for him. He was known for praying for long periods of time although no one knew what he was praying for or why he looked so sad while doing it. Whatever it was he prayed for, everyone respected him for his leadership and the faith he represented to them.

How would anyone know that his past held such horrors? His wife knew only bits of the pain from his past. She came with the old pastor from Northwest Ohio and moved down to Columbus, Ohio leaving their past and stories behind. Adam Byrd accepted an offer to work at his uncle's church. He and his wife Jenny moved down to Columbus after she finished High School.

Adam's Uncle married Adam and Jenny in his church with almost everyone he knew attending. There was only one person he knew that was not there and he knew why. It broke his heart, and as much as he wanted to say something, he knew better.

They had a good life and after a year of teaching in the church to the youth, the young couple decided to go to college for a bachelor's theology and Divinity. They both were outstanding students and always made the dean's list. They both held unique insights that their instructors enjoyed hearing.

When they finished their schooling, Jenny had a bachelor's degree in theology, and a baby on the way. Adam had gained his Master's in Divinity with honors. Everyone was proud of them and he was excited when he was asked to start a sister church in Cincinnati, Ohio.

That is where Adam, the new pastor eventually became the grey-haired pastor. Years later, the day came that his oldest son Scott had followed in Adam's path and graduated from college with a Master's in Divinity. Later that day, he found his father sitting in the back of his church, which is where he liked to sit.

He always said it was where people like him tended to sit.

That same day is when Scott asked what he meant by "people like him." Scott knew that the people who sat in the back of the church were those who felt they didn't belong. Many times, the newcomers had fallen so far from grace, they simply didn't know where else to go.

Adam with his lifetime of wisdom told Scott to sit and pray with him. Scott never told his father no on matters of praying. So, they sat there in silence and heads bowed. Then as if the words came from nowhere, Adam spoke. "I have not always been a man of God. When I was young, I counterfeited money and my best friend was a drug dealer. We had a lot of good times, but the day it all ended, I lost my best friend.

I remember one time when we got ourselves into some trouble. My friend Scott and I had just printed our first batch of perfect twenty–dollar bills. I mean, they looked like they came from the U.S. mint. You see, you were named after my friend Scott Bearman. I will get into that later.

The guy who trained us to do it and helped set up the operation was out of New York City. From what Scott told me, he was part of the mafia and needed a place for their operation with less people watching. Since Scott was selling drugs and running a network of dealers, his contact from New York decided to trust us, a couple of dumb kids.

Scott was making money from his drug sales, but he wanted something I could do and not get hurt from. We worked hard to learn what needed done and Scott lost a good amount of money as we practiced. Then came the day that a few stacks of fives and one-dollar bills got washed, dried, and reprinted to twenties.

Honestly, I was excited and so proud of what we did. I remember Scott saying how much easier things would get. He was right too. I gave up my part time job, and Scott stopped going out to sell drugs. Instead, he would just distribute to his intimate network and focused on what he called his little empire.

Then Scott decided we needed to test the money in public. That is when the first problem happened. We were told by the people in New York to never spend any of the money locally. They said it would get back to us and mess up the whole process we had going.

That left the option for us to go to Canada. Windsor was only a few hours' drive. We could gamble, drink, and have a wild time. To two young guys with not a care in the world, it was the greatest idea either of us had. That was until we were twenty-four hours into our stay. You see, when you are betting a high and the wrong people notice, things can go wrong quickly. That is the day I learned there were criminals everywhere you go and that is the day we met Edwin.

Edwin didn't seem to be much of anyone. He talked like he ran a large operation of illegal gambling, car chop shops, and a few other things. It sounded impressive, but like I said, he didn't seem like much of anyone other than the kind of guy who liked to talk big. Most likely we thought he told stories about his boss and made it sound like it was all him.

Scott thought the same thing and tested Edwin with asking to get us into something exciting. Then he showed six thousand in twenties from the backpack he carried to make a point. Most people would ask why two teenagers have that kind of money. Not

Edwin, he just assumed that we came from rich families.

What Edwin took us to was an underground fight club. When we got there, it was after the first match was over and a guy was cleaning up the ring. The smells of the place were hard to pin down. Different people smoking different things. The truly rich were in a protective area, while average folks were in a standing-only section along the ring.

We were led to a private area where the higher bets could be made. There would be three more fights that night. We placed a thousand on the first fight, fifteen hundred on the second fight, and twenty-five hundred on the third fight.

Each bet was for the underdog of each fight. Scott told me later his thought was to see how well the money got taken. If they lost the money, then no one would be upset. That was a good thought until the third fight was actually won by the underdog. The guy had horrible odds and only won because the other guy slipped and fell.

You should have seen the look on Scott's face when he realized we won the big bet. Then came time for the payout! We tried to leave without a word but got stopped by Edwin. He was excited for us and said the guy running the show wanted to see us. Normally we would be excited too. That was, if we hadn't pumped several thousand dollars of counterfeit money into his bank.

Edwin showed us into an office with a guy who looked as though he had been in a few fights himself. While we slowly entered the room, Edwin didn't pay us any attention and walked to the guy behind the desk. He was very cheerful saying "These are the guys I found. I knew when I met them, you would want to have them here."

There was no way to miss the two piles of money. Both piles looked to be made of twenties. This added concern for me, and I had to think it did for Scott too. Either way, this didn't feel like it would be a good meeting with a good ending.

The boss behind the desk stood up and pointed us to the chairs on the other side. This blondish brown–haired guy stood six foot six and twice the size that I was. To say it gently, he was not someone you wanted to upset.

As soon as we sat down, Scott looked at the money on the desk. He had to be thinking about all the scenarios that could happen. My thought was only on one scenario. Scott smiled and asked if all the money was our winnings, and how much we won.

The boss guy walked around the room and in a deep voice answered Scott. "Yes, that is all your money. There are five thousand in one pile and the other pile is ten thousand. If things go the way I want it to go, you will be taking the ten thousand pile. If it doesn't go well, then you will learn what happens when you cross the wrong person."

I didn't have a smile to begin with, but Scott kept his. Then Scott took a step that I would have never done. Scott told the boss guy that he knows why they are there and wanted to know how he figured out what we did. It was odd that he was admitting we did something wrong, but he would not say what that was.

Edwin on the other hand looked confused. He also looked scared when his boss pulled out a snub nose revolver and put it on the desk with the nozzle pointed towards us. The next thing said was by Edwin trying to defuse the situation. He was not permitted to say much when his boss told him to shut up till, he was ready to deal with him. I could of only imagine that Edwin bringing counterfeiters to the underground fight club would not be good for his health.

With all the tension, I finally broke and asked what would happen to us. I was thinking the end result would be Scott and I being shot in the back of the head, then dumped in some alley. Either way, I did know that we would not be happy with the end results.

I can't say what I looked like, but Scott started to laugh, and Mr. Boss guy stood up. After he stood up, he said" Call me Francis. I am not going to hurt you; I want to use you. These bills you guys used are good work. The stack of real money is all yours if you can tell me who made them and how I can get a supply."

It was unreal. The gun sitting on the desk, the two stacks of cash, and a criminal boss trying to buy the money we made. It felt as if we were in some kind of pulp fiction novel. I was more confused and scared than I had ever been. Francis was upset with Edwin, but happy he found us.

"So, what is the deal with the gun? Why are you threatening us if you want us to help you?" I had to ask and expected an answer. That was till Scott jumped in by saying that we would be happy to be his middlemen. We would not tell him who made the money, but we would take one percent as an administrator fee. Francis acted like he was thinking about it till he grabbed the snub nose and pointed it towards Scott.

There was not much we could do. If I tried to get the gun, we both would have been shot. Scott was starting to show some fear and put up his hands to show he was not going to do anything, and then asked what good shooting us was going to do. He tried to joke, but his voice didn't portray humor very well. Scott said "Look, I don't know if you think we are asking too much, but we need to make money off the work we are going to do. It is not like your guys work for free."

After letting Francis think about it a little, Scott continued with saying "Plus there is another issue with shooting us. This looks like a nice rug and furniture. I hear it is horrible getting blood out of fabrics."

Aftermath (Bearman Series)

The alley started to look like the end results again, but for some reason, that didn't happen. Francis instead put the gun back on the desk and sat down. I could see some fear in Scott's eyes, but his voice seemed to go back to his normal cocky sounding way.

The two of them talked about fees and order sizes. Edwin and I stayed quiet till it was all done. Scott was talked down to a quarter percent and protection when he or I were in Windsor. We would be the only contact Francis would have. The first order would be for twenty thousand in twenties. He wanted to mix the money with the payouts for the fights and other deals he had going.

There was never a question that Scott or I were innocent, but now we had gotten ourselves involved with another criminal organization. This meant to me that we would have two different groups that would be happy to kill us if they were not happy with us. Later I found out that Scott told his contact in New York City what happened and cut him on what we were getting from the quarter percent.

Finally, everything was settled, and we knew that we had three orders. One delivery a month of twenty thousand. We would get eight dollars for every twenty-dollar bill. That meant eight thousand plus the quarter percent for our cut. We would drop off twenty thousand and come back with ten thousand dollars. After expenses and paying the guy in New York, we walked away with three thousand five hundred per delivery.

Everything was going well, and we had ended up making another agreement to extend the deliveries till otherwise notified. After Scott had made a few deliveries on his own, I decided to go with him for a little fun on a delivery. What I didn't know was that Scott had started to bring drugs down from Canada. I guess he wanted to make the trip worth more.

We drove up to a town called Port Clinton that sat on Lake Erie and took a boat that took us to another boat. The second boat took us into Windsor and Francis would meet us the next day. Scott explained to me on the boat that Canada had a hell of a drug problem. Since people had to wait so long for medical treatment, they would try to find other ways to help with their pain.

Scott continued explaining that his New York contact had supplies come in from Canada, so he decided to use Scott to bring them through in a less monitored way. Scott seemed to enjoy doing it and it explained why Scott was giving me all but five hundred of the profit.

I was unsure how Scott found it fun. Scott knew I was not a fan of anything stronger than weed and I have never changed my thoughts on that. After everything that happened on that trip, I would never forget having a real glimpse into the dark side of the world, one that I never thought I would be part of.

I know it sounds foolish. I was counterfeiting money and working with a guy who had a small drug empire. At least that is what he liked to call it. But I didn't think I was hurting anyone, so I was not a criminal.

So, I listened to Scott tell me about what has been going on in Canada. He had found people who thought he was some dumb kid and underestimated him. That allowed him to make a network of connections. The problem I had was that the people he told me about sounded as dangerous as the mobster from New York City.

Then things got strange when we pulled up to the docks in Windsor. A guy looking like he had lived a rough life stood on the dock waiting for us. I first realized that this guy was not someone they were expecting when the boat captain grabbed a gun and Scott pulled out a 45 that I never knew he had.

The guy on the dock must have realized or knew what was happening. He lit a cigarette and after he exhaled the smoke from his lungs, he put up his hands. Scott was the first to get out and talk to the guy. Then as fast as things got hairy, it was as over and seemed to be back to business as usual.

The guy turned out to be one of Francis's guys. Scott was expecting Edwin, but this guy was sent instead. Since everything seemed to be fine, we grabbed the bag of money and went on our way. The whole event gave off a spooky feeling. Between the creepy guy and the foggy mist that rolled in, I was expecting something bad to happen. Even the lights of all colors filling the city didn't seem bright enough to chase out the darkness.

As we followed the guy to his car, I asked Scott what was going on and where Edwin was. It turned out that Edwin would be meeting us at Francis's club. He had another job to do before coming and escorting us around. This guy was just getting us to make the exchange. And that all appeared to be OK. That was till we got to the car.

It was a four door maroon Lexus. The guy told us to hand over any guns we had on us. If we didn't, we would not be going to see Francis. The smug look on his face went away quickly when Scott said, "No problem, I am not going then."

It only took a few steps of us walking away when the guy caved. With the guy agreeing not to push for Scott to give up his gun, we got in the car. It was odd to watch the buildings go by and not notice the excitement of the city.

Before, when we were in Windsor, the excitement of the casino was amazing. The gambling, free booze, all the people, and all the noises made the place seem magical. That magic that made for an exciting tale to tell was gone.

Now the buildings we passed didn't give off a feel of excitement, but rather a feeling of loneliness. It was as if I began to see the true cold side of what I was doing. I was not just someone breaking the law. I was part of something big, something that reached out in all directions. It was something that had no end.

What we did was push others down so we could move up.

Scott and I had a kind of power that was addictive. Scott might have known it and accepted that. That might be why he always looked for more ways to get in deeper. Scott didn't just start selling drugs, he built an entire network of people that sold for him.

Me on the other hand, I only got into helping Scott because of the money. The power that came with what I did, that never crossed my mind. I didn't even think about it until we drove through downtown Windsor on our way to meet a crime boss. All this was happening because I made counterfeit money.

I was doing a lot of thinking and not much talking, and it felt like we drove for an hour. In all reality, it was maybe a twenty-minute drive when we pulled up to an old brown brick building. It was the same building we were at the first time I came to Windsor. The same building where the underground fights were held, and Francis had his office. I don't know why I was expecting to be driven to another building.

Maybe the first time I showed up, all the excitement made the building look mysterious and exciting. Now it looked gloomy, worn, and the kind of place you would not be seen in during the day light. The only thing that looked new was the door. The nicest thing I could say about the building, is it should have been torn down.

This time, we didn't pass the fighting ring. Instead, we were lead down a hallway with barely any lights. It was so dim, I tripped over something and about knocked Scott down. That got Scott yelling at Francis's guy about the darkness. It was not hard to see that Scott was getting upset with everything.

Then as we got to Francis's office, Scott got himself so worked up, there was no question that something was going to happen. For some reason, Francis was in the same kind of mood. As we stepped through the office door, Francis called Scott a son of a bitch. Scott didn't hesitate and laid into him, asking why he sent his "steroid loaded chimp to strong arm us?"

Normally, this would be just an awkward situation, but out of the five people in the room, four had a gun. That would leave me as the only one without. All it takes is one person to think too much and pull out their gun and then everyone pulls out their gun.

What happened next shocked me. Scott pulled out his gun and sat it on the desk, then he sat down. When Scott sat down, I sat in the chair next to him. Francis put his gun on the desk as well and waved off his guys.

The anger was still visible between them, but the tension seemed to have gone out of the room along with the goons. Scott spoke first. "You're pissed and I am pissed. We either need to work this out and do business. If you want to end our arrangement, we can go our own ways."

Francis could only smile to Scott's comment. It was a cocky teenager telling a grown man who had spent a lifetime of crime to get where he was, to shit or get off the pot. Even though most adults would be upset by this, Francis seemed to relax, and in a nicer tone began to talk again.

"Scott, do you understand the value of a relationship? I am not talking about what ever slut you find for a night or two, but a real relationship built on trust. Like the relationship between your friend next to you and yourself.

You trust him and know he will be there for you. He might be scared, but he looks like the type who would fight for you if he had to. Do you realize we are building a relationship? A business relationship. Something I hoped to expand on. Something we both could have made lots of money on.

Instead, you went to Tim Wilkins, and that is why we can't do business. In fact, I can't let you do business with anyone in my town now. Normally I would just run you out of town and tell you that I will have you killed if you return.

But with you Scott, you don't seem very good at listening to good advice. You know, like the kind that tells you not to return. So, I am left with one choice and you or your friend will not like it."

I knew what that meant, and I had to imagine Scott did too. Since I felt I would be dying that night, I spoke up. I told everyone that I would not be dying. Then I told Scott that we needed to just leave before this jerk thinks we will take him seriously.

I honestly thought Scott would have gotten up with me. Scott just sat there looking at Francis and I didn't say anything. But Francis kept looking at me then back to Scott. He and Scott had both put their hands on the desk and were resting them a few inches from their guns.

"So, are you going to do it? I expect you're the kind of guy who only does the dirty work when your left with no choice. How about we...." before Scott said anything else, Francis yelled out a name. Once the name was called out, both of the thugs came in with their guns in hand. It was not long from that point that we were dragged back out the door and down the dim hallway. Then out the front door we went where a white contractor van was sitting. It didn't dawn on me why the van stood out to me. It was doubled parked with the side door open.

By the time I realized that the van was waiting for us, we were being thrown into it. After the two goons climbed in behind us, I heard one of them tell someone in the driver seat to take us to the construction site. Then a loud banging of the door shutting made me that we were not going to get out of this without a miracle.

The driver of the van didn't say anything, he just drove. The goons on the other hand had no desire to keep quiet. They told Scott that he should never have crossed their boss. They kept talking about the first time that we went to the fight club. They had told us how they thought we should have been taught a lesson that night.

This went on for ten minutes or so when the van pulled into an unpaved area. When the tires of the van went from the road to the dirt, you could hear the difference. The gravel and dirt under the tires made some sort of popping or crunching noise. It is a sound that you don't mistake and you pay attention more when you know why you are there.

You know in the movies, there are so many scenes where the criminal takes the guy, he plans a place to do the deed, the killing. I remembered one movie that had taken place in a construction site. The guy about to be killed had his hands tied and was led to a pit with a steel beam sticking up. The guy was thrown in and they poured cement on top of him.

This was nothing like that. Our hands were free and the site was for a one story building. Nothing so grand or scary about it. It all seemed more like one of the tense deals Scott had taken me to before. That was till we saw the driver was Edwin.

That bastard walked in front of us and whined about how bad we made him look. It was interesting how none of these guys acted like they had seen a mobster movie or show. With all the talking and not restraining us, and then standing so close to us.

Let me tell you something that my uncle used to tell me. He always said, "If you let the devil get too close to you, he will take every chance to whoop your ass." That always stuck with me. That night it was my saving grace.

Edwin got right up into Scott's face and when he did, Scott punched him in the nose. The two stupid goons were stunned and watched Edwin rolling on the ground holding his nose. While they focused on him, I donkey kicked the guy behind me. When I looked over to Scott, he was trading punches with the other guy. It didn't look like Scott would win that fight on his own.

Edwin was crying and the guy I kicked was holding his crotch. They both had dropped their guns to the ground. Scott was starting to look as he was about ready to give up. So, I did the only thing I could think of and picked up one of the guns.

I don't remember if I have ever held a gun before that day, but I haven't since. When I pointed the gun and pulled the trigger, the bullet hit the final goon in the hip at point blank. The sight of it has stuck with me. Blood and flesh exploding out with the bullet. How the guy I shot moved when he got shot, was nothing like the movies.

The guy I kicked pushed himself up and ran to his friend. As much as I was in shock about what happened, I knew that I had to get Scott and myself out of there. Scott must have thought the same thing because he grabbed the other guns and started to walk off. If I didn't help him, he would not have gotten too far.

Much of the rest of that night was a blur. Scott had us meet with his contact named Steve for the drug exchange. He said that would be the only why we would get out safely. We could not go back to the docks. Francis's guys would most likely be waiting for us.

When we got to the meeting point, we told our story. Steve said that he would take care of us. We gave him the guns and Scott handed him an envelope of money. I could only wonder and guess why the goons did not search us for weapons. We didn't have any, but still. There were so many things they could have done different and we would have been dead.

Steve came back after an hour to tell us that he set up a mule to get us back to the States. We would also be taking the drugs as planned. Then Steve got close to Scott and told him "My boss will not let this go and you can tell your boss that we honor our protection agreement."

After that, we were driven down to Leamington by a guy who didn't talk during the hour drive. At least not to us, but he did grumble and talk to himself. So, when he pulled up to a rocky section that met with Lake Erie, we didn't say anything to him as he pointed to a boat. We did what we thought we had to and got into the boat with a different guy.

The captain of the boat took us to a real boat and then to Marblehead, Ohio. Once he dropped us off, we were on our own. We did the only thing we could and Scott contacted his guy Mick. Mick was to meet us in an hour, and that was the end of one of the worst nights of my life."

Adam's son just sat there with his mouth open. The story he just heard changed everything he thought he knew about his dad. He knew the pastor who led his community to stand up against crime. He was the pastor that the Mayor would ask for advice and prayed with the local high school football teams before every game.

Finally, Scott Byrd spoke and asked "Why, why did you tell me this? No one would have known this and now people will run you out of town." Scott Byrd had a look of such fear on his face while his father began to smile.

Adam looked at his son for a short time studying him. Then he said "You can tell whoever you like about my past, or you can tell no one. This is your choice, but my choice led to three great kids and one of them is about to go off to teach a community. You need to know that not everyone is good, or evil, and some have a past that leads them to an unusual future."

Neither the father nor son said another word to each other the rest of the day. Scott accepted his father's past and used the story to help him teach others. Adam retired as a beloved pastor and never told any of his children about really happened to Scott Bearman. He would only tell them that he prays for his friend's soul every day.

Chapter Four

For the Love of it All

No matter how you look at your past, you find it directing where you go. Some will let those events drag them down and hold on to them. Some will hide the past and make choices to not allow others to know what has happened. Then there are those who hold their past close, show the world their anger and fight against the evil they have found.

Rose was one of those who found a spirit to fight. After learning of her fiancé being killed in what everyone said was a drug deal gone bad, she fell into a place of depression. While her friends and a friend of her fiancé had tried to help her, it was her friend Jenny that pulled her out.

When Jenny pulled Rose out of depression, she jumped into anger. Not knowing what to do with that rage she felt, it came to her to use her brain.

Rose was not going to fight the drug world that took Scott from her in any other way. It was in the late evening that she was sitting in the apartment that she and Scott shared, that she found a glass in front of her. She had filled the glass with what was the last of bourbon left in the place.

Jenny and her fiancé Adam had come over to make sure Rose didn't drink too much and go crazy. She was normally a calm person, but Adam was Scott's best friend and Scott had told him how Rose could drink too much when she was upset.

With Scott gone, Adam felt it his responsibility to watch out for Rose till she got back on her feet.

The three of them talked about all the things they could remember good about Scott as a way to bring back their friend, even if it was only in their memories. As Rose shivered from the sip of bourbon, the warmth filled her. Then she stopped the conversation. She told Jenny and Adam that she was accepted at Ohio State University in Columbus.

Jenny jumped up and gave Rose a big hug, then told her about how she and Adam would be moving down to Columbus so Adam can work at his uncle's church. The two girls talked about what they would do and how great it was they would still be close together.

All the plans they made changed as Rose dove into her studies to become a lawyer. Jenny and Adam spent much of their time at the church or working to make extra money. They did try to meet up, but what was planned to be a weekly event, became a biweekly, then a monthly event. All the way up till Jenny and Adam moved out of Columbus to start a new church, they kept the monthly visit.

By that time, Rose had met a new man in her law classes. They both graduated at the top of their class. They both had been so excited and so were their families. It didn't take long for the two of them to decide to get married. Rose wanted to be open with her new fiancé, and she told him everything about her first fiancé.

That night, they told each other of everything they could think of.

With no secrets left to tell, they got married, had a daughter, and both became very successful in their fields. While her husband went on to become a corporate lawyer, Rose became a lawyer for the Department of Justice. She tried to help those who have gotten themselves in too deep. She also went after the heads of organizations or people that held some sort of position.

Then one day, as she was interviewing a guy for drug trafficking, he said a lot of things. It was not till the guy was asked to give up his boss that the fear on his face told them a lot. When he said, "All I will say is, he will kill me and not in a quick way."

This comment was nothing new to her. Almost everybody starts it off with that same comment. They tend to build up the danger to do one of two things. First, they wanted to say they didn't give up anything. They would feel proud of themselves. Those who say this are those who don't know anything. They tend to be low-level guys.

Most times, it was the low-level people who said this. It was not that they didn't know something. It was that they knew so little, they were useless. The useless want to feel as they had more value than what people see in them.

The other set of people who make this comment is building up a deal. Those people know they have something and want to get something for it. This guy had something, and he wanted a big deal for it. That is why he smiled and followed up his comment with "But you know, I would be willing to tell what I know. Just tell me what you are willing to give me for what I got."

Rose had played this game several times and knew how it would go. That is why she started with "You know I am federal? You know transporting drugs and illegal guns across state lines is a federal crime? So, you are aware, this means you will go to federal prison."

Sitting back in his chair, the guy smiled and leaned forward, and demanded a deal. Just like Rose expected. Now she was ready for her big surprise. "Let me tell you something, I won't cut you a deal. That is, unless you have something really good, I mean it has to be very good. You see, my counterpart in New York is interviewing the people who loaded up your car.

After you left, we ran a raid. We found guns, drugs, and things that make me sick.

If the guys busted in New York turn over the better information, they will get the deal. Then you will have ten years behind bars. I don't care either way."

Rose began to stand to walk out of the room. This must have been what made the guy shout out "I can link John and the others in the Martinelli Family to everything." Out of anything he could have said, this was what she had always wanted to hear. Rose knew of John. She had heard his name and knew he was a big deal when she was in high school. By this time, John had become the second to the top of his organization.

"How can you do that?

What do you have that will connect John to the drugs, the guns, and all the illegal things he is involved with?"

Rose sat back down and stared at the guy with an intensity that would put fear into any man.

However tough the guy thought he was, at that moment his voice cracked. He requested a deal in writing before he would say anything.

What he didn't know was that he could ask for anything and get it. The only thing he had to do was help put John of the Martinelli family away for life.

It took a little more than a day to get the deal wrote up. Once Rose had the deal in hand, she put it in front of the guy and told him to sign it.

While he looked over it, she began to check the camera and voice recorder. She wanted to make sure that nothing was missed and there was no question about what was said.

Finally, he signed the deal, and Rose signed to make the deal official. She looked at the contract. She could not help to think it was funny that an Irish man with the name Kevin Doyle was working with an Italian crime family. That thought passed quickly and the interview began.

After several hours and a few breaks, the interview was finished. Kevin was swept away to an unknown place. He now was in witness protection and till the trial, he would not be heard of again.

Rose worked closely with the New York office. Some would have said that Rose was running things from her Ohio office. With all the work she did and the information Kevin was providing, she expected to shut John's business down and not leave room for someone to take it over.

Then came the day one of the people from New York had an attempt on his life. That was all it took for him to back off. In most cases, that would have slowed down what was going on.

John would have been able to rebuild and put up new walls to distance him from the ever-closing grasp.

What John didn't know at the time was Rose was not going to let things slow down. The people out of the New York office already knew Rose was the brains behind the case. So, when the lead guy took a long vacation, nothing stopped.

It took another two weeks before John found out who was really running the show. Then another week after that for Rose to hear that a contract was put out on her. The word on the street was that three hitmen had accepted the offer.

Two of the men who were expected to have taken the contract had left New York City after having a meeting with John. They both were under investigation for some murders. They were not working together, and it seemed to be the first to the prize gets the money. One of the guys was last seen going to Pittsburgh, PA. The other guy wasted no time and went straight to Ohio.

The third guy was an unknown man. Rumors had always been going around about a group of high-end fixers. These were the people who could fix any problem and would for the right price. The only reason it was believed that one of the members of the fixers took the contract was because of John. He liked to brag and when he would use his fixers, he would tell people the fixer is on the case.

No one knew who these people were, and John would not say a thing more than they are his fixers. He would almost glow when said they were doing something for him. It was almost as if he had a sense of pride.

With all this news, Rose's family went into protective custody, while Rose pushed on and got closer to John. Then on a late night, while Rose was walking to get some air, she went to a park next to her house. She thought she would be safe with the protective detail in the car watching her.

It was not completely dark, but more of that dusk time of day. Rose passed a few people and after a little bit, she noticed two men walking behind her.

It was not the detail assigned to her and she was in a place that she could not see them. Instead, when she looked over her shoulder, the two men were wearing hoodies on an evening a little too warm for hoodies.

She was about to run when a guy walked past her and towards the two guys. Her belief was that the guy that just passed would notice the guys chasing her and help.

So, she did it and ran as fast as she could. Rose expected to hear the sounds of the guys running after her. Instead, the two men laid on the ground holding their sides.

Rose didn't stop running and ran till she found her security detail walking around looking for her.

The next day, she found out the guys had been stabbed in their legs. They confessed to being hired by a guy with a New England accent. They didn't get a good look but gave all the details of how they were to meet him after they had Rose.

The two guys had become more scared than they ever thought possible. They should not have had any issues picking up a skinny woman.

Instead, they had been stabbed in the legs. The knife went down to the bone. So, when asked how to find the guy that hired them, they happily told the police.

It only took the police a few hours to mobilize. They swarmed around an old house that looked abandoned. What they did not realize was their target was not inside the house.

Instead, he was in a hotel about two miles away.

So, when the police bashed the door down, they only found a homeless guy strung out. Once the homeless guy saw the raid, he curled into a ball and screamed "I didn't say anything, I didn't say anything. Please don't hurt me again."

After that, the police took the homeless man in and questioned him. No matter what they tried to get out of him, all they got was how he was only waiting for the aliens to come to get him.

In the hotel where the was staying, he was not alone. His guest was one of the third hitman. This was not something you normally see. Hitman don't tend to spend much time with each other. That means nothing good would come of them being together.

As they talked, the guy who hired the kidnappers sat in a chair with his hands tied behind him. In fact, he was restrained at the legs and chest as well. He knew that no matter how this visit ended, it would not be good for him.

He was right, too.

From behind him, he heard his guest speak. "You know I heard about you. How sloppy must you be to have people know who you are? I mean you are a person of interest in several cases of murder. That is unprofessional. I mean, you give us professionals a bad name."

Then his guest walked next to him and the metal chair. "Let me help you out. If I don't, you will get yourself killed or you will hurt the wrong person."

The next thing the hitman knew was how much pain shot through his entire body.

All he could see was a white light and hear the blood rushing through his eardrums. This was because he just had his right hand—pounded to the chair with a bible that broke his fingers and the joints.

Tied to the chair crying and wailing, the lesser of the hitmen were left in the room by himself.

It was not long for the other people in the hotel to complain about the noise. After the third call, the hotel manager went up to investigate.

He didn't expect to see a man tied down to a chair and bleeding when he entered the room. The manager got two steps into the room when he saw a gun and some papers with Rose's information all over it. He knew that he had seen a lot of strange things in his job but was out of his pay grade.

The hotel manager didn't want to get involved or release a dangerous man. So, he ran back down to the front desk and called the police. It was a great day for the two cops that showed up.

Aftermath (Bearman Series)

They were about to arrest a man wanted in connection to several murders.

When they walked in, the man was passed out. The pain had got to him and knocked him out. The cops called the ambulance once they made sure he was alive, then called their dispatch to ask the dispatcher to run the guy's background, only to find out that he was considered very dangerous.

That caused the hotel to have more people in it at one time than it had ever had before. The amount of police who came to the scene, were mostly there to see a real hitman. With his hand damaged and all the evidence in his room, he would not be able to do anything to anyone.

The would–be assassin found himself waking up in a hospital. He thought about his career and tried to get up to run. Instead, he found his left hand had been handcuffed to the bed and his right hand wrapped.

Once he relaxed to think things through, he noticed he had no pain and felt quite euphoric. He knew instantly that he was feeling the effects of morphine. Once that realization dawn on him, he began to yell. "NURSE, NURSE, I NEED SOMEONE NOW! HELLO, IS ANYONE THERE?!"

A nurse and officer walked in looking at the guy. In a calm voice, the nurse said "Mr. Thrine, what is wrong? Are you in pain?"

He quickly replied by telling her that he is a recovering addict. The nurse looked puzzled for a moment and the officer told her to remove the morphine drip. The officers' instructions made her realize he was a junky and she rushed over to remove the needle from his arm.

Removing the morphine, she informed Mr. Thrine that he would be in an immense amount of pain when the drugs get out of his system. Nothing more was said as she ran off to get the doctor.

"Why am I handcuffed?

I was the one who was attacked.

Why is she calling me Mr. Thrine?

I am..." The officer stopped him before he could go on. "Mr. Thrine, I don't know who you were about to tell me you are, but from the three driver licenses we found, only one was real.

That is the one for a Carl Thrine, who is wanted in connection to several murders and a list of other crimes? We also have witnesses that have identified you as organizing the attempted kidnapping and assassination of a federal employee."

Not another word was spoken for the remaining time Mr. Thrine was in the hospital. The doctor explained to him how his right hand was so damage that, he may never have full use of it. It was hard to accept, but he did. He knew that he had done the same kind of torture to others. Not every job he took was to kill someone.

This was his big break into what he thought was the big time. By working with a real crime family, he felt this was, a group of people that would give him respect.

This job was what he thought would be where he really was able to make a name for himself. Not just knocking off someone that no one noticed was gone.

The thought ran through his head as he was being transferred to the police station. He was dealing with his pain and trying to handle it as best as he could. When he was at the police station, he was fingerprinted, and put into an isolation cell.

Everything was ready to formally make the charges known to Mr. Thrine. The only thing they wanted to do was see if they could get him to confess.

If they could get him to tell who took out the contract and give the details, Rose could go arrest John. It would be over, and she would have done with the biggest case of her life. Rose would have put the man she felt was responsible for the death of Scott Bearman behind bars The death of her fiancé from High School was Scott Bearman.

The police wanted to let this guy sit in the cell and speculate what was going to happen. He already knew they had his real name, and this also meant they had his outstanding warrants.

Carl Thrine was running through everything he had done and who had paid him to do it. He was working on two lists and looking to figure out what he could get leverage on for leniency.

Since he didn't kill anyone in Ohio, he began to think he was safe from the death penalty there.

The other states where he had committed a few hits had a death row penalty and they could transfer him there. The thought of that scared him more than anything else.

As he got deep in thought, an officer delivered the food. When Carl looked through the viewing window, he froze and didn't touch his food. Then he said "I know you. How do I know you?"

The officer just smiled towards Carl and said "I am just a Revenant. I'm someone you don't want to see, and if I see you again, you will learn about true pain firsthand. Now eat your food and make sure NOTHING is left."

After that, the officer walked away and fed the other prisoner. Carl sat on his bed with his tray of food and noticed a small piece of paper.

It was clear what was being done. He was being given a warning. Now he started to question how safe he was and where could the family get to him.

Carl didn't know that John's organization was not very strong at that time. In fact, John was doing everything to keep from having another group push him out.

When Carl opened the piece of paper, he read it.

I found you in your hotel.

I know more about you than you know.

I have an offer for you. You are to ask for a lawyer before saying anything.

If you don't say anything or make any deals with someone who mentions my name, I will let you live. No one will come after you and you will not need to look over your shoulder.

–Revenant–

There was no chance he would let this note be found. He had heard about these kinds of notes. They tend to be a one-time offer. Not the kind you take for a joke. He just thought it was an urban myth, something whispered by a few criminals.

Now there was no question of the note, and he would definitely not say anything. So, when the police took him in to be interviewed, he didn't say anything other than he wants a lawyer. Rose watched the whole five minutes of the interaction, wondering if she could have gotten something out of him.

Carl went back to his cell and Rose started to walk out of the police station. She was about fifteen feet from the door going out when she saw him.

Her body would not move.

One of the protective detail guys bumped her not realizing she had stopped. Then in almost an inaudible voice, she said "It can't be him."

The protective detail started to look around for threats. After they realized there was no threat, they asked Rose what was wrong.

It was only a fraction of a second that she saw the officer who was the same one that served the food to Carl. She didn't get a good look at him either.

She knows that the person she thought she saw wouldn't be a cop.

Instead of believing her eyes, Rose assumed that she was imagining things. Once she had herself convinced that she only saw a ghost, a memory that worked its way up, she began to move. Then Rose and her detail walked out of the station.

The sun was bright and the warmth from it gave a comforting feeling. It was two days since she walked out of the police station. Rose knew she almost had John where she wanted. Then the contract on her life would be gone.

She knew from the little information she had been given was that John was involved. If she could get Carl Thrine to spill the beans, John would not just go to prison, but never breathe free air again.

Even with two more hitmen out there, she figured the police would catch them just as they did Carl. She didn't know how the police had found Mr. Thrine. It didn't matter, Rose would not let anything destroy her day.

That was till Rose and her protective detail began walking to the SUV. Walking into the parking garage was not like any other time. They walked down the sloped drive that led them under the office building.

When they got just out of the sunlight and got to where all the cars were parked, one of the detail guys made a comment to his partner.

"Where is the guy in the booth? This place always has someone in that booth."

Both of the guys on Rose's detail grabbed their guns and moved Rose faster towards the SUV.

They got close to the SUV doors when a guy about 5'8" stepped out from behind the rear of the SUV.

That is when the guys on both sides of Rose fell to the ground. The percussion of the gun put Rose in a state of shock. Without a thought, she covered her head and sat on her heels. The only thought that ran through her mind was how could she make it out alive. What would her husband do when he found out she was killed?

The gun started to lower towards Rose. Then someone tackled the shooter. Rose looked up at the sounds of the men fighting. This time, while looking at the men, there was no doubt in her mind.

It was Scott Bearman in front of her. Her heart raced and all the memories of them rushed back. She forgot about the hitman for a while. That was till a loud scream came from one of the two men fighting on the ground.

Only Scott stood up and the other man laid on the ground, dead. The sounds of heavy breathing were all Rose could hear. She looked into Scott's eyes and broke down.

After all these years of mourning him and all it took for her to move on, she now is faced with the truth.

Rose had faced his death to only have a living dead man come back into her life.

"Listen, there is not much time. The gunshots will draw the police and I can't be here. I want you to go home after you are interviewed by the police. I will meet you there."

Scott didn't wait for Rose to answer. He left the same way he ran in. This time not so fast. Then he was gone again, but she knew that it was not the last time.

Her mind was running wild about what could have happened that Scott was alive. There were so many possible ways that he could have been there to save her.

Rose let her mind go as far as it wanted and stood in place quietly.

She was not sure how long it was when the police got to her. It was the screaming sirens coming down the parking garage ramp that brought her back to reality.

For her, everything went so fast. The police saw the scene and her standing there surrounded by dead bodies. First, she was questioned as the area was blocked off.

Then she was led away from the scene and taken home.

Rose felt as though she was being treated like she had been violated. The officer that took her home searched it looking to make sure no one was there. He and his partner looked everywhere they could think. When they found nothing, they told Rose that they would be parked out front if she needed anything.

Then they were gone.

Now that she knew she was safe in her home, Rose dropped to the floor. In the middle of the living room surrounded by pictures of her family; she fell asleep.

It was a tapping of a foot that woke her up. The sun was starting to set and the light coming through the windows had an orange glow.

A strip of that light was shining on the tapping foot and the man doing the tapping.

Scott leaned forward with a smile on his face. "You know you never were to see me. Since you have, I owe you the truth." Scott paused to allow Rose to get up and get herself straightened up.

Rose went and got two glasses of bourbon along with a little food. As she walked past Scott, she handed him one of the glasses, all the while saying "I picked up drinking this stuff after you died. My husband knows I drink it because of you, and he knows about you. Well, as much as I did until today."

Scott took a sip and smiled. "Makers Mark! You didn't just pick up drinking my drink, but my brand too. I must admit I still drink this to remind me of you and the past."

The glare from Rose's face told him to leave the past where it was. So, he went on and told her what happened the last day she saw him. The day that Scott Bearman died.

He explained how Dan was killed, and Mr. Stone took him to work with him and his organization.

He divulged how the only way he would do any work for John as if he agreed to a deal. It was a simple deal of him never going after anyone from his past and agreed that his former friends would all be safe from his reach.

After a few years, John forgot the deal and didn't think about it when he came to take the contract.

After all, Scott had done several jobs for John. The organization Scott had become part of was a high-end fixer firm. They prided themselves on being able to fix any problem.

What John didn't realize was Scott made Mr. Stone aware of their deal. So, in a revised contract they made to renew John's membership with the firm, the clause that John would not harm, contact, or contract someone to affect anyone from Scott's past got added to the contract.

Finally, Scott told Rose that she needed to go and talk with Carl Thrine. Not letting Rose ask too many questions, he told her that he will not say anything till he knows the Reverent approves.

Rose had so many more questions but felt as if things made sense again. She didn't say a thing when Scott got up and went to leave.

Before he did leave, he looked around the room. He saw all the pictures of her and her family. There was one picture that caught his eye. It was a picture of her husband with a young boy.

"I am so glad you didn't name your son after me. I know Duke did that with his firstborn. I mean Adam, well you know what I mean.

You have a good life.

You are well known for what you do, and people expect you to be going places. I don't want you holding on to my memory. You have great ones being made here.

Now I have to catch a flight and you need to get to Mr. Thrine to get him to talk. Either way, John will not be a concern for anyone by tomorrow morning."

He didn't leave time for any more discussions as he walked out of Rose's life again.

IT ONLY TOOK ROSE A few minutes to realize what Scott meant by his final comments. She ran up her stairs and got herself around. Then she ran to the police cruiser to find the guard asleep inside.

With a few knocks on the window and opening the passenger door, Rose got in and the officer woke up with a scare. "I will tell you what. If you get me to the station on Cleveland Ave., I will not tell anyone you were asleep while guarding me."

Knowing that he would be in a lot of trouble, he just nodded and asked how fast she needs to get there.

When Rose told him that she needed to be there now, the lights and sirens came one.

The other cars that pulled overlooked like a blur and in no time, they were in front of the police station.

Rose didn't say anything while getting out. Not till the police officer thanked her for not telling anyone.

She told him "Don't worry, I won't tell. I have too many criminals to worry about rather than an overworked cop." Then she shut the door and began to run into the police station.

She was stopped by the desk Sargent.

After showing her identification, He let her pass. It took a few minutes for her to find the detective in charge of Carl's case. Of all the things he could be doing, she found him drinking a coffee and eating a doughnut.

He knew of Rose and what she looked like. He had been pouring over the file of the guy trying to kill her. So, when he saw her, he walked over to her to see what was so urgent. Rose was not in the mood to be placated by this guy. She had dealt with enough detectives that see a young woman and get stupid thoughts. She had shown them all to be wrong. Well, all but how beautiful she was.

Before he said anything and while she was walking up to meet him, Rose began to loudly tell him that she needs to talk to Mr. Thrine.

Of course, he didn't think she could do anything. So, he gave her a list of why it would not be safe for her to see him and how a woman like her should not be around people like Mr. Thrine.

This didn't sit well with her. So, she took a step closer and made sure she was close enough that he would feel the heat from her breath. Then she said "Listen, I have put away more pieces of crap than you have ever met.

I have looked almost every one of them in the eyes. I am about to put away a mob boss, but you think I am too sensitive to talk to Mr. Thrine. Is that what you are trying to say?"

That is all it took, and he walked away mumbling. He had had an attitude, but he was also told off by a woman that he thought he could tell her to go away. What surprised him was how Rose got the district attorney down to the station in the same amount of time that it took him to get Carl Thrine into an interview room.

Getting everything, she needed in hand, her body was pumping with adrenaline. Then she walked into the room where Carl was sitting at a metal table with his hands cuffed.

She gently put the contract in front of Carl. As he looked at it, he wondered what she was doing there. Why would the woman he was trying to kill put the plea deal in front of him?

He didn't wonder anything after what he heard her say. Rose got close to him and cupped her hand so no one could read her lips. Then she said "Sign the damn deal. My friend promised me you would. You might know him as the Reverent."

Carl's eyes got as big as they could, and he began to shake his head to acknowledge that he would.

That was all Rose had come to do.

She had what she needed. Now she would send the New York office to go after John.

It took less than a day to get the raid set up. Rose had even flown into New York to see John in person walking out of his home in cuffs.

Thanks to all the information provided by Mr. Thrine, there were a lot of people being arrested. Not only John's empire would be crashing, but Rose would be overseeing about twelve other cases. Some of the people were just starting to become a threat and others had already made a name for themselves.

This had made Rose's career. She had started to become a legend. None of that was on her mind. Rose was only focusing on the raid on John.

Then it all began.

The swat team went into the house and moved through it showing off their training skills by not leaving any rooms unchecked.

Rose's heart dropped when she heard on the radio that John was found. The problem was that John was found on the floor dead. He was shot three times in the heart.

The overweight man was laid out with three bullet holes in his heart. The reports and news articles made it seem like John of the Martinelli family was killed in a way to be disgraced.

Many people that day felt deflated and angry that John would not be sent to prison. What seems to have been forgotten is John would do well in prison.

His world revolves around being at the top of the criminal world. A mob boss in prison will have respect and privileges.

Rose was one of the people that day upset that John would not see justice. She also knew what no one else did. John was killed by Scott Bearman for coming after her. She wanted to believe that John was given the justice that Scott knew would be more serving.

Instead of going out as a King, John went out scared and no one around who cared about him. He knew in his final moments that everything he built was gone.

Later, Rose was asked by a reporter what she thought about John and all the raids that took place that day. It was reported that Rose only said one line.

"All the Kings Fall"

Chapter Five

Becoming a Hero

Changing your life is a big thing at any age. Mark left his life in Fostoria, Ohio after his brother died. All that was left for him back there were a few people that remembered his name.

His grandmother passed during the height of fire season and his mom overdosed on a mixture of drugs.

He never did make it back for the funeral. In fact, Mark didn't know about it till after he got back from putting out a wildfire.

Mark was a smoke jumper, or a wild land firefighter. He worked his way up the ladder with education and hard work to become one of these elite firefighters.

To Mark, this was his way to make the world a better place.

The harm he caused in his hometown weighed on him. He felt responsible for his brother's death, too. His brother Jay was a bad kid and got himself into a lot of trouble. Then Jay became violent, causing him to pick a fight with the wrong person.

Jay was killed by someone Mark considered his closest friend. Even after all that happened. Mark knew that his friend killed his brother because there was no one else who had a reason to do it.

Even though Mark felt he knew who his brother was killed by, he didn't know all the details. Mark thought about his brother regularly. He thought of his family and few friends he lost.

It is hard to be young and lose so many people so close to you.

Then a year after he officially became a smoke jumper, someone Mark knew from back in Ohio had come to visit him. This was the first time anyone from Ohio had come to visit.

Normally having a person from your past stop by when you thought no one knew where you were is a happy surprise. Now, having a friend from your past who was said to be dead, is more than a shock.

When Mark got back from two days out in the woods, he had a message saying.

"It's been a while.

How about you join an old ghost from your past. I have a bottle of Makers Mark like the old days."

The only additional information was an address. The short message was enough for Mark to know who it was. He dropped everything he was holding and stood there with his mouth wide a gape.

First, he wondered if it was a joke. Maybe he said something to someone about his past. If it was his old friend, then it was indeed an old ghost. One that he thought was killed years ago.

As much as Mark would have liked to ignore the note and think of it as a very bad joke, he went to the address listed on the note. He drove down the streets he had come to know so well. He pulled into a hotel that he had passed for what felt like hundreds of times.

Once he stood in front of the room listed on the note, he froze. He wondered what he was doing, why was he falling for this joke. It will probably be a few guys from work.

If he were to guess, it would be Jerry.

Jerry was always doing things like this.

Finally, Mark walked back to his truck without knocking on the door. He decided he needed to think about what he would say. If this was his old dead friend, he needed to be sure of what he would say.

Hundreds of scenarios played out in his head. Just as many questions came up. When he started to get his mindset on how he would act and what questions he had to know, a knock on the truck window surprised him.

Mark jumped and about hit his head on the top of his truck. Once the shock of being caught off guard passed, he had the real shock.

He was looking into the eyes of his friend. The friend that had been killed several years back and got burnt to a crisp in his own truck.

He did try to talk, but no words came out. It was not as if he would be heard since he was still in his truck. Mark got out of his truck after the man or specter jerked his head to say follow me.

That was all it took, and Mark followed the man who he knew could not be there. Once he caught up with his friend, the first question he asked was what most people would ask a dead friend. "Scott, how are you here, aren't you dead?"

Scott Bearman, this was the guy who took a small-time drug dealing dual to having a name back in the farm towns of Northwest Ohio. The same guy who had gotten into a fight with Mark's younger brother and most likely killed him. The same guy that Mark missed most of all walked next to him.

Scott just smiled in the odd way he does and said "I had a job to do about two hours out of this town. I normally have a week of free time between jobs, so I came here. Let's go into my room before getting into any great details."

It had to be hard for Mark not to let all his questions out.

Scott acted like this was not a big deal, but for Mark, his world had just been changed.

Walking into the room, Mark watched the door shut behind him and let everything go. With all the questions, comments, and random thought, nothing could be properly responded to.

"Mark, I know you have a bunch of things going through your head, but let's sit down. We can have some bourbon and catch up. I have one day left before I go back to my life."

Not to wait for Mark to answer, Scott got up and got them both a glass to drink out of.

While Scott poured, Mark put his thoughts in order. Then he asked some real questions. "What do you mean back to your life? I have friends on social media from back home. They told me that you were shot and burnt inside your truck. You are dead. Jenny told me everything. You know Jenny, she married Duke."

Scott took two or three sips of his drink before answering. When he did, he talked about how Mr. Stone appeared. The tale of the group out of Michigan, and how Dan had tried to get him arrested.

Then told him about everything that led up to the last day he was in Risingsun Ohio. How he had to do some bad things. How Dan was the one found in his truck. With all that was told to Mark, he went on with the telling of how he became what Mr. Stone called a Fixer.

Scott tries to cover every detail that would put Mark at ease. Then said that he has a name people in some cities call him. They both laughed when he said, "I am the Reverent."

Mark asked through laughter "so you are the ghost? I guess I was right when I thought I was looking at a ghost."

They laughed and talked about the old days back in Ohio. All the memories came flooding back to them. The littlest detail sparked a reaction. From looking at them, you would swear they had not been this happy in years.

It was great for them both.

All the pains of the past were forgotten. That was till Mark asked about his brother. "Scott, I know you said you didn't kill my brother. What you really said was Jay was not killed by your hands. I need to know if you had anything to do with his death."

They sat there looking at each other without a word for about fifteen seconds. Then Scott told him the whole truth. "I did and I was there when he died. Now don't think I was happy about it, but your brother was trying to kill me. He sent a girl that had mistaken my guy for me and stabbed him."

After that, Mark stopped Scott from giving any details. He didn't need the details; he knew enough of them. Mark had gotten what he wanted to know all those passing years. Learning that he was right about everything was all he needed.

His brother went out to become something he didn't want to see him become. Mark and Scott talked of their past lives. It became clear to both of them that the other had a strong hand in who they had become. They played off each other's choices and happily faced what came from it.

"So, last time we talked, you were about to come out here. The big firefighter and it looks like you became what you set out to become. Something had to happen since you got out here. When I asked around about you, people talked like you are the local hero."

While Scott was asking this, he got up to get a menu so they could order some dinner. When Mark noticed what Scott was doing, he picked up his cell phone and called a restaurant he knew well.

Scott just watched and listened as Mark placed his order. Mr. Liu, can you send me two of my usual to the hotel on Wilson? I am meeting with an old friend from back home." Mark shook his head as if the man on the other end knew he was doing it. Then he finished the call with "Yes sir if he is in town long enough, I will bring him over. I know he will love your place."

With the phone call done, Mark looked and noticed a puzzled look on Scott's face. "OK, let me tell you what is going on. I am a local hero. I didn't want to be, but it just happened. It is also how I met Mr. Liu's daughter. I don't know if you heard, but I am engaged."

Mark started to smile at that statement. It was clear that he was in love and happy. Things for Mark were looking good. He was who he wanted to be. A man that is out saving people and risking his life to make a better place.

After a moment of Mark thinking and smiling to himself, he started talking again. "You see I got out here and kept to myself. I didn't want to get wrapped up in anyone's life.

I was focused on the classes I was taking and the work I was doing at the Station.

Then a little past a year of being here, I was getting groceries when some thugs were harassing a woman walking down the street. She looked like she had just gotten off work and was trying to get home. And you know, there are rules we had. Being a man, I had to stand up for a woman in need.

That is why I put my groceries in my car and went to help. I didn't know that this town had an issue with a gang, but I did after my next move.

I shoved one of the kids and watched him fall. He took his buddy down with him. They looked like they had watched too much television and wanted to be like what they saw.

After knowing you and seeing the things we did, I doubted these guys would last around us back then.

They didn't even look like they could fight and they were skinny. They had no muscle tone or muscles to be seen.

I didn't realize it, but that is how I started everything. I changed my life. I picked a fight with two guys to save a pretty girl.

I actually just smacked them around a little and kept pushing them. A group of people watched it all happen. After that, I thought it was over."

Pouring some more bourbon into both of their glasses, Scott asked a few questions while Mark sipped on his drink. Scott mostly wanted to know when Mark became a fighter.

They joked about that fact for a bit and Mark went back to his story. "You see, I didn't realize that one of the people watching was part of this gang. This guy was not happy about someone making his guys look foolish.

E.A. Maynard

I wished the girl good luck and walked away. I didn't think anything about some of the people watching me walk to my car and drive away.

I realized later that I should have paid attention.

Since I found out everything, I came to think everyone could be watching me. The best part is to me, it doesn't matter. I think that there is someone always watching us all. But that is me. The point is this guy got my plate number and saw what I drove.

About two weeks later, I found myself faced with one of the guys I smacked around plus another two guys.

These guys did look like they could fight. They weren't skinny and had muscles.

They started talking about what happens when someone makes a member of the gang look like a fool. It didn't take much thinking to know where this all was going to lead to.

Now, I don't know if you knew this, but after I started selling drugs, I kept a little 22 revolver on me. I did everything I could not to let anyone know I had it.

It was my last resort. I didn't tell you in case you came after me.

Don't take that wrong, I didn't think you would, but I also see what happens when you lose it.

So, when those guys started to walk towards me and pulling out knives, I grabbed my gun. These boys were not going to be whooping my ass.

They also thought that it was a game for them. You know the type, the ones who played too many video games and lost the ability to notice the difference between the real world or a video game.

Luckily for me, a cop drove by and saw what was happening. I even got luckier when the cop pointed his gun at the gang bangers.

They got arrested for attempted assault with a deadly weapon. Come to find out, this was not the first time, but state laws made it the last time for a long time.

As good as I felt to be out of that and that the state has a stand your ground law, I knew that it would not be the end of it. If that gang got upset that I smacked around two of their guys, how will they feel that three of them are now going to be locked up for several years.

I talked with the cop that helped me out and when I told him I worked at the firehouse, he seemed to like me more. We decided to meet up and he would fill me in on the gang. He would also invite the girl he was dating from the firehouse.

As he went on his way, he did tell me that he loves seeing people stand up. If that is what he thought, what did others think?

It took a few days for us to meet up. At that time, I went to work at the station. I met his girlfriend and we talked a bit. I will say it was good to talk with her. I hoped her boyfriend would be as good to talk to.

Honestly, I was wanting some friends. I don't know if you have any friends now, but it was hard on me. So, when we did meet up, I knew the girlfriend Katie well and felt like I knew Matthew. The three of us must have talked for about three hours at a restaurant called the Dalian King.

The food was good and towards the end of our first time hanging out, Matthew told me about the gang that I seemed to have pissed off. Come to find out, the guy running it was from some South American country with ties to the cartel. His full name was Santos Jesus Ramos Nolasco.

This guy was only 5' 6" and the police had been trying to get him for the rape of four different girls. What pissed me off was when I heard the girls all were younger than thirteen years old.

Scott, let me tell you. At that point, I would have tried to kill that Santos. I just pictured this creepy guy who made women cringe at his touch. My stomach turned at the thought of this guy.

I was not one to say that everything happens for a reason before. I do think that way now. As I walked out, I saw that girl from before. The one who the two thugs were bothering. I almost went back in, but I decided against it."

Scott stopped Mark with a joking cry out of "why didn't you go get the girl?" Scott would have only done something like that around his closest friends. It got them both laughing and took away the tension Mark was building.

After they finished with a few more jokes, Scott asked what happened next. It didn't take Mark long to get back on track. When he did, he went to where he first met Santos Jesus Ramos Nolasco, the child molester.

"I hate to say, but I lost track of time at this point. Things seemed to move at such a fast rate. The day that Santos was sitting on the back of my car, he made it clear that he planned to kill me.

Me being me, I didn't like that plan. That is why I decided to channel my internal Bearman. In my calmest voice, I told him that his plan has some flaws.

Then I said "It might be that I am in a good mood today so I will tell you what those flaws are. I come from a place that people have tried to kill me and I am still here. If you come after me, you have to ask which one of us will be here in the end."

He obviously didn't like that. My guess was that no one really talked to him like that. He liked it less when I went too far and in a voice loud enough that anyone could hear, I told him to leave the little girls alone.

I learned that child molester doesn't like to be called out. At least he didn't like it and he tried to show me how much. The worse thing was how he tried to fight.

He started to bounce around with his fist up, telling me how he was going to whoop my ass. I noticed people watching again. This group looked to be bigger than the last one.

As I said, I was channeling you. That is why I did a move I had seen you do before. I took a step closer with my hands open and up. When he bounced closer to me and pulled his fist back to punch, I smacked him with my right hand and held onto his face. With extending my right foot and posting it next to him, I pushed him to the ground. I turned with as much force as I had

His legs flew up in the air and he made a thud sound. It had to of hurt. There was no question that it knocked the air out of him. People must have known who he was because a few people cheered. The excitement was something else. I finally understood how you let it get the better of you.

If two guys didn't run up to help him, I would have most likely kept going. Instead, they picked him up and started to drag him away. One of the guys pulled a gun and pointed it somewhere in my direction.

People ran away when they saw the gun. I don't blame them. Who wants to be shot by some thug that can't aim? Well, I guess no one wants to be shot at all.

While Santos was being taken away, he yelled back that he was going to kill me. I didn't expect him to stay around when I heard the police sirens.

Man, I will tell you I didn't want this; I wanted a peaceful life. Maybe meet a good girl and have a kid. Now to do that, I had to deal with a gang leader."

Mark started to smile as he thought about what he was about to say next. It was one of those smiles that says I have a secret. Scott had no idea what was going through Mark's head, but it made him happy to see that smile.

Then after a few seconds of being lost in his thoughts, Mark went back to telling his story.

Aftermath (Bearman Series)

"After the people walked away and I went to get in my car, I heard a voice that sounded so sweet. It was this beautiful black hair, Asian woman. The same one that I had stood up for and the reason all this stuff was going on. I only could look at her and felt a smile covering my face.

We looked at each other and she started to blush.

I knew it was not just me that was feeling the excitement of being this close to the other person. It felt to me as the world passed before another word was said.

She broke the silence by thanking me for helping her out. We talked for about a half-hour. It was the best conversation I had in a long time.

There was nothing more than talk the whole time. I had to imagine that the people passing by were wondering why we were there talking. Whatever they thought didn't matter of course. There was a beautiful woman in front of me and her focus was on me.

Scott, you know I am not a bad-looking guy. On the same note, I am also never going to be modeling anything. That might have been part of the reason I didn't want to let it end.

Her laughter was music to my ears. When she invited me to come to the restaurant, I didn't even think when I said yes. I did make one request and that was that she join me for dinner. She got a smile on her face and nodded her head.

We had our first date set up. I didn't think about it being in front of her father and friends working at the restaurant. I won't go into that story; I tend to go on about the three-hour date.

As you know, that was not our last date and as I said, we are engaged. I guess she really liked me, or she is going a long way to say thank you."

Laughter filled the room as Scott started to laugh uncontrollably. Scott interrupted Mark's story and his laughter by saying "Man you're a dumb ass. You're not a bad-looking guy and to be my friend, you had to be a good person to walk away when everyone else was trying to get what I had.

You were and are one of my closest friends. I knew you always to be honest to me. So, you relaxed and let a girl see how you truly are.

Why the hell would she not want to be with you? Don't put yourself down. You have done a lot more than most people we grew up with. What a life you have, I only wish I could have had this."

Mark was filling with a good feeling. He had just been given the highest praise he had ever gotten. He was about to thank Scott for what he said, but there was a knock at the door.

Scott jumped from his seat and pulled a gun that was hidden on his ankle. Walking over as though he was expecting to have something happen, he asked who it was when getting close to the door.

A woman's voice came through nice and clear. In that sweet voice that Mark knew so well they heard "I have an order from the King of Dalian." Mark pointed to Scott and mouthed to put away the gun.

Of course, Scott did it and opened the door. Scott was stunned by how pretty the woman was. Her Raven hair was pushed back, but just resting on her shoulders seemed to bring out the smile on her face. With a soft expression that made you want to trust her, she asked for Mark.

Mark was already on his feet and pushing Scott out of the way. Scott was happy to see his friend hold someone he really cared about. He was starting to feel guilty for showing up.

After all, Scott has done nothing but destroy things while his friend has been building and saving.

Everything seemed to brighten for Mark as his fiancée walked into the room. She carried two bags of a dish that neither Mark nor Scott could pronounce. It didn't help that they had too many drinks, too.

It didn't take long for Mark to take the food and ask her to sit down. The only time Mark appeared to be acting strange was when he went to introduce Scott.

When Mark said "Laura, this is my friend from Ohio. Sadly, he is only in town till tomorrow. Laura this is..."

That is when Scott jumped in. "Thomas, but my friends call me Tom. Laura, it's good to meet you."

Mark gave Scott a funny look but went with it and referred to him as Tom as long as Laura was there with them, which was no longer than twenty minutes.

While everyone was in high spirits and laughing, Laura said goodbye. "Tom, it was good to meet you. I will let you boys talk. I have to go study if I want to get my master's in accounting."

With a big hug to Scott and a bigger kiss to Mark, Laura was out the door. The closing door just made its thudding sound when Mark and asked what was with the name change.

"So, do I call you Tom or Scott? What am I missing?" Mark waited, then Scott explained it to him. "Hey, don't think I was trying to play games.

Remember Scott Bearman is dead. He died back in Ohio by Dan as far as everyone knows.

That is the day Thomas Norris was born. Since then, I have not been called by Scott other than by you. Well, there was Rose, but that was because I had no choice but to let her see me."

Mark smiled and shook his head. "Alright TOM, you will have to tell me that story sometime." Scott gave a smile back and told Mark that maybe after he finished his story.

"Ahhh yes, I was just about to go on my first date." They both opened the dinner that Laura dropped off. Mark showed his food and pointed at the food, then kept talking.

"This is what we had.

It is an off the menu item. I guess there are a few dishes that are true Chinese dishes that can be ordered if you know them. I can't say any of them. I sound like I am having a stroke when I try."

Mark tried to say the dish name they were eating, and he was right. They laughed and Scott almost choked from laughing while eating.

"Laura and Mr. Liu were good to me. It was the first time I felt good about being here. Don't get me wrong, I was excited about becoming a smoke jumper and what I was doing while getting there.

Those two welcomed me in and treated me well from that day forward. That is why I didn't have any questions when I asked her to marry me.

But before then there was still that Santos guy who I knew wanted to do something to me. I made a choice to stop letting him come after me and to get rid of the scum bag.

I was not going to do what you would have done, but I needed to tear down that gang and have them out of my life."

Scott knew what he would have done back then. He was just wondering what Mark thought. So, he gave in and asked. "Let me ask you something. What do you think I would do? I mean, I was not that bad, was I?"

Mark could not help to smile. "You know I watched you give Dan his scare. I also watched what you did to the guy who attacked you back in Fremont.

I guess that is where I got part of my plan from."

Scott replied with "So you're saying that I had a little mean streak in me? OK, I can see that, and I guess some others would too."

Mark lost his smile for a moment and reminded Scott that he killed Dan and had a part to do with his brother's death. A mean streak was an understatement.

It took a little talking about what happened with Mark's brother Jay. The tension had gotten very heavy till Mark let out a deep sigh and told Scott he knew that he did what was needed. If it was not him that killed Jay, someone would of. They both knew Jay was on his way to do a lot of things much worse than he had.

"So, what do you mean you got your idea from what I did? If I was in your shoes now, I would just put a bullet in the head of the gang leader and the next two in charge." Scott said with a smirk.

Mark got back to the story.

They had eaten all their food and filled their glasses of bourbon back up. "I went to my new friend Matthew. I told him what I had planned. He didn't like it, but what I was going to do could break that gang up, he would help.

Aftermath (Bearman Series)

All I need from Matthew was a ride to the house of Santos Jesus Ramos Nolasco. The catch was I needed a ride in his police cruiser. You know how optics help makes a point. The gang needed to know I was friends with the police.

The next time Matthew went on duty, I met up with him and we went to Santos's house. It made my day to see about ten guys on the porch with Santos. I really wanted others to see this. The word needed to get out to the other gang members.

You could see the cockiness in his eyes since he had guys there to have his back. When I stepped up to the chain-linked fence around his front yard, he started to talk.

Santos was almost yelling to make sure everyone heard him. First, he told me how foolish I was to come to his house and how the cop with me would not save me. Then he finished his crap by making a joke that made no sense.

Hell, his guys didn't laugh till they heard him laugh.

I knew what I came to do, and I refused to get wrapped into his rants. Instead, I calmly said, "Santos Jesus Ramos Nolasco, you should know who you try to mess with. I have learned who to be friends, with so when you do something, you can walk away."

I pointed with my thumb over my shoulder to Matthew. Then I told him that I would make him a deal. I gave him a week to break up his gang and get out of town.

He jumped in asking me what would happen if he didn't and came after me and my friends. That got me to smile. I said with a smile "If you don't leave, I will burn down your house and every house you stay in. I will burn down anyone's house that tries to keep the gang alive. Now if you come after my friends, I will make sure you can't get out of the house. Anyone that helps you will suffer the same fate."

I walked away at that point.

He was saying something, but the fear was clear in his voice. I don't know what he was saying, and I didn't care. I have given him the warning and that is all I needed to do.

I waited for a week and a half before I checked if he was still in his house. It was late when I did, and I saw him in his house drinking with a few guys and some girls.

I expected him to not take me seriously, so I went back to my car. After digging around for about a minute, I found the pipe wrench I needed.

Returning to the house, I found the gas meter and turned one of the connections till some gas started to come out.

It did take some work, but it did what I needed. Gas started to spray everywhere. It was more than I was hoping for. I didn't wait and I found some brush along with the house and got a nice little fire going.

I didn't want to be around to be identified and left before the fire got to the gas. I knew well enough what was going to happen. This would make my point and send the message to get out.

At least that is what I thought. Hell, it worked for you. Instead, I came out of the fire station to see my car on fire and Santos next to it.

You remember my old car, it was nothing fancy, but man I liked it.

Santos didn't see me right away, but when he did, I was running to put the fire out. With one of the stations' extinguishers, I got the fire put out, but my car was gone. He made sure the interior and engine all burned.

Before I had a chance to think or say anything, I was spun around and punched in the face. I fell, but oddly, the punch didn't hurt. It was being caught by surprise that knocked me down.

When I got up, you could see that Santos looked to be on the edge of tears. As I was about to fight him, he started yelling. "You burned down my house. I have nothing and now I will end you!"

That is when he pulled out a gun and pointed it in my direction. From how he was holding the gun, I had to assume he never shot anyone from a distance. He had his knuckles up and the gun sideways. I never understood why people do that. Anyone that has shot a gun knows you can't aim like that.

No matter how he held it, one lucky shot could do some damage. I try to talk him down and pointed out that if he tries to kill me, there would be no way out. The building has cameras and was full of people.

One of the guys I worked with must of saw what was happening and came out to see if I needed help.

When he yelled my name, Santos turned to look and pulled the trigger.

I don't know if someone had been praying for me or I am lucky, but the shot missed me. The bullet hit the inside of my car and put a hole in the burnt headrest. I took my chance while Santos was thrown off by shooting the gun.

He must have never heard of finger control. I turned sideways and rammed my shoulder into his chest. We both went to the ground this time, but I kept control of him and with a few elbows to his face, he was done.

At least I thought he was.

Santos laid on the ground looking bloody and defeated. The building residents started to come out to see what they could do to help. I saw a police car down the street.

My body was sore, and, in my gut, I had a bad feeling. Turning to look back at Santos, he had his gun back up and pointed at me. I don't know why people feel like explaining themselves, but I am glad for those who do.

He was telling me what he wanted to do after he killed me. He pushed himself off the ground and looked me in the eyes again. This time I was too far to do anything. The cop pulling in the parking lot, on the other hand was not.

The officer got out and saw the gun in Santos's hand. From that point, things got dicey. The officer pulled his gun and yelled for Santos to put his gun down.

Santos just looked back at the cop and smiled.

With one last look Santos's looked into my eyes and said, "Let us end this" and pulled his gun back in my direction. As far as I could see, one of three things would happen. The first would be that Santos would Shoot me and the cop would shoot him.

Secondly, the cop would not wait for Santos to try and kill me. He would just shoot him to save me. Finally, Santos puts down the gun and gets put away for attempted murder.

With the smile on Santos's face, I didn't see the last option happening too much. What happened was he pulled the trigger on his gun and missed me.

The cop didn't miss Santos. It took Santos just a few moments before he fell to the ground.

I only heard Santos fire his gun, but I saw a mist of blood come from his back. I was told that the Officer put three bullets into Santos.

After all that had happened, the local news picked up the story. They told people that I stood up to the gang and that caused Santos to come out after me.

They made me and the officer that showed up into heroes. We were the talk of the town for a while. Now I am just someone the neighborhood knows. I am OK with that too.

There was an investigation over Santos's claims that I set his house on fire. I don't know if John the investigator was really looking or what, but I do know he lives in the same neighborhood as I do with his two daughters.

So, when he came back saying that the fire showed no signs of arson, I was relieved.

When someone asks me about what happened and how could I stand up to that gang, I simply tell them I just did what was right. Since then, I have gotten known for being a firefighter and a member of the smoke jumping team. In time, people stop talking to me about the gang and more about my job. I am well known and a part of the community.

I am not sure what people consider more when they think of me, but here I am known for good things.

I ended up going on more dates with Laura and that lead to us being engaged. You saw her, you can see how lucky I got with her. She is smarter than she is good-looking, so I look at my life as being a good one.

We just got our first house.

It is a nice fixer-upper, but the bones are good and the house is in a great area. Laura is already talking about us having two kids."

That got Mark and Scott to Smile. They talked and joked about Mark being the hero who got the girl. They talked about as much as they could. They both knew that the end was coming. It will also be the last time they would see each other.

They both started showing signs that they realized this, too. It was hard for them because of how much they missed their friendship. Then it happened.

Their laughter ended in sighs and long pauses. As if they were trying to find something more. The problem was the sun was coming up and Scott had to go.

"Mark, we both know I got to go. Don't worry about inviting me to the wedding, I will be there in spirit. I see I have nothing to worry about with you. You became the good guy you wanted to be. I am the villain that people expected me to become. That is why I won't be back. I would only bring you trouble.

Just do one thing for me.

Don't tell people that I was here.

Remember that you met with your old friend Thomas Norris. It would not be good for either of us if the wrong people found out I am still alive."

Scott and Mark got up without a word, hugged, and nodded to each other and walked out to their vehicles. Marked watched as Scott pulled out of the parking lot. He felt the same pain as he felt when he heard Scott died all those years ago. As a tear rolled down his cheek, a smile followed.

It comes to his mind that he was given a gift to see his friend one last time. Scott took the risk, whatever that was to see him one last time.

He fully realized that Scott and he were real friends, friends that would be friends no matter what.

Chapter Six

Going Solo

Do you know why people wait so many years to make someone a saint? It's because all the people who knew the bad crap they did are gone. I am not trying to have you think I am a good guy. In fact, I am as far from being a saint as possible.

When I went by Scott Bearman, I sold drugs, ran a prostitution ring, shacked business down, and even killed.

I am not all bad though. I had friends that I would do anything for.

They were like family. I still try to keep tabs on them when I can.

Then there was a girl I wanted to spend the rest of my life with. I did everything I could to make her happy and tried to keep her out of the darker side of my life.

The last day of Scott Bearman being alive, I killed someone who pretended to be my friend while informing the police on Me. The day I was given my revenge on him was the day I learned that I could never come back.

By the time I was out of Ohio, the news of my death had spread. That is how I became Thomas Norris. I also started a new life as a fixer. Not the kind of fixer you hear about in the news. Those are more like a spin doctor or a public relations professional.

What I walked into was taking care of someone when they knew something they should not of. There are times I need to send a message.

Sending these messages as was asked of me, made me lose any issues I had about taking a life.

After some time, I began to develop into a real professional fixer. I also got to know lots of the secrets of those in public office. I still remember a couple from Arkansas whose husband held some highly elected positions. They always wanted to make the hits look like suicide.

I did a few of those jobs but then they switched to a different group of fixers. I would read about what was done and it was clear that the media called it suicide or accidental death. But I never heard of anyone shooting themselves in the back of the head.

That is when I realized that Mr. Stone had trained me to do more than just kill. He made sure we thought through what we would do and that it would achieve the set goal.

A good example of this would be a job I took in North Carolina. It was the first one I got to choose and do on my own. I was going to go down to the Carolinas to find a guy who stole data from a corporate client of ours.

I didn't ask what data was stolen. To be honest, whatever it was had nothing to do with what I needed to achieve. All I needed to know is that the company was a security firm with an office in Raleigh. That office is where the data was stolen from.

One of the pieces of advice I was given by my mentor Mr. Stone was to start following his transactions.

Before I went down to Raleigh, I spent a few days looking at where he spent his money for the last two years.

I found that there were two places that this guy would go enough that he felt safe to return to.

With two likely places to start looking for the thief, I was off to go down to North Carolina. It was time to make my first target feel the pressure.

Since Raleigh was less than a day's drive, I skipped the flight and took my Toyota LAND Cruiser.

With a few modifications, it ran fast and had plenty of places to hide my guns.

The other benefit was that it didn't stand out. No one would normally look twice at me or what I was driving. That was important to me.

I let my hair grow out a little bit, so I looked more like what everyone my age looked like.

I did find it funny that I was going down on my birthday to do this job. Not Thomas Norris's birthday, but the day I was really born on. The day Scott Bearman was born.

Maybe I consider this my birthday present to myself. My commission for this job was eight thousand dollars. That would give me a good dinner and a nice, overpriced bottle of wine. The rest would be stored up. Mr. Stone has told me a few times that it is smart to save up for a fire sale.

As I pulled into Raleigh, I was singing happy birthday to myself and talking to no one but whatever ghost might have been riding along. Then I worked my way down to 40 and Lake Wheeler Rd. It was a mostly residential area with parks and some businesses.

The reason I had come down here was my target had a friend in the area. There was also a credit card purchase in the area leading up to when he stole from his company.

I guess I should give the guy a name. I can't tell you his real name, but we can call him Frank. That is as good as a name as any.

Frank showed a tendency for parks and wooded areas. This area had plenty of those around. I just needed to see if anyone had seen him at one of the parks in the area.

It took me three days before I found out that Frank was going to the Carolina Pines Park. It was a nice park and I enjoyed being there. I found myself watching the sunset through the trees.

Then after a few days, Frank walked by me. He looked as he did in his picture. He even was wearing the same blue button-up shirt and a haircut like a twenty-something, but it was easy to tell he was past his twenties. He was a fast walker, not like most people in the park. Most people tend to either slow down and try to enjoy what was around them or they would be there for a jog.

Frank was doing neither.

I thought he was at the park to get away from the stress. When I followed him, I found he was going to meet a girl. At first, I was hoping that he would be making a drop, but I saw them kissing and begin to talk while holding hands.

It's hard to truly speak quietly when you're excited. These two were the perfect example of this. They would start to talk at a volume hard to hear, but by the third word, I heard everything. When they finished talking, I could have been twice the distance away and still hear what was being said.

Frank told this girl that he would be going out of town that night. He then said he would meet her out at his cabin on the lake. I was wondering why Frank would not just have the girl go with him. What was going on that they had to meet at another time?

Then it dawned on me.

Frank told the girl that he waited to make sure it was safe, he told how he escaped the building and slipped through the fingers of security. He was playing spy and they both were getting off on it.

It got to the point that the two moved off into the woods for some romantic time. I was going to give them a few minutes and walk off, but they finished in about five minutes. From the sounds they made, the spy games foreplay must have gotten them close before they went into the woods.

As they pulled themselves together and made enough noise breaking branches and rustling up the ground, they would not have known if someone walked up to them.

E.A. Maynard

That is when I walked back down the trail to my car. I knew the area Frank parked, so I could follow him and retrieve the data. This seems to be an easy job. A little work and a nice payout.

I expected Frank to go somewhere close by. Instead, he took me on a forty-five-minute drive out to B Everett Jordan Lake. After a while, it got hard to follow him and not be seen.

The good thing was I knew where his cabin was located. So, when we got off of route 1, I went towards the dam for the lake while he went on to his cabin. It was a small place and nothing special, just a one-room place with a wood floor.

I waited for about two hours to let Frank get settled and relax in his cabin before going over. I figured he let his mind run about being followed and someone coming after him. All true things, but to him, it was his mind running wild.

The good thing was his cabin was back a mile-long road with no one else living within two miles. If you didn't know about Frank's cabin, it would be unlikely you would see it. I learned about it from a property sale that happened eight years ago. Then about a year later, Frank applied for a building permit and it was approved.

It's amazing what is public records. What the public records don't tell you might have gotten me killed. Being on the property for the first time, I didn't know if he was a prepper and has trapped all over or was, he was just a guy coming out to fish.

I had known a few preppers growing up and they all seem to be loaded up with guns and could hold up in a secret bunker for a year or more. From what I gathered on Frank, he was an outdoors man, but not a hunter.

Then as I found the cabin, it dawned on me. He was getting off on playing these spy games in his head. That means he would have picked up a gun to finish the persona of being a spy.

When I got up to the cabin, the dark brown wood had some patches of moss growing on it. I could only guess the place was not kept up very much. The windows had a white film of a material that I didn't recognize. The exterior was not well taken care of, and the windows could not be seen through.

Going to the door, I noticed it had a board to help stop the wind from getting in. The problem was the door was made to open outwards. Unlike most home entry doors that swing inwards, I would not be able to kick in the door. I would have to figure out another way to get to Frank.

It might have been an hour when it came to me. I was going to try a reverse of a gag I saw in a movie. In the movie, a guy knocks on a door and the door swings out hitting him in the face. The difference here was I knew the door swung out.

Frank pushed open the door when I knocked on the door. When the door open, Frank stepped out with the door. That is when I pushed it back into him. When I did that, I heard an "ouff" and what sounded like he had dropped something metal on the wood floor.

After a few more times of slamming the door into him, I let the door swing open on its own. Frank laid there looking as if we had gone a few rounds. It was a sad sight to see. A grown man being taken down with such little effort made me wonder how this guy made it through life. I could have also had a rougher life than most, so my judgment might not be the best on this matter.

It was not doing me any good just having him lying there to recover. Pulling him up to his feet, Frank started to whine and plead for his life.

I expected a fight from this guy, but instead, I got a guy who used a fireplace poker to defend himself.

When I dragged him to the center of the one-room cabin, I saw a large rolling suitcase in the corner.

The inside of this cabin looked to have everything you could want. It had indoor plumbing, electricity, and a gas stove. I realized the exterior was a disguise. He must have wanted to think that he had a real get-away- from- It- all cabin.

It made sense though.

After listening to what he was saying to what I assume was his girlfriend, made him seem like a person I should have been worried about. Instead, he was just a guy who watched too many spy movies.

After a bit of Frank asking questions and crying, I had looked in what I thought were the obvious places he could have hidden the information. I turned to him and started to talk with him.

"Frank, I am going to explain what is happening once. You will listen and tell me what I need to know. If you do this, I can promise you will live. The people who have the contract for you have put a requirement of the data to be returned. You are being brought in alive as a bonus, but not a requirement.

Now, I want to know what you did with the data. Where did you put it?"

Frank quickly replied with "It's in my suitcase under my underwear! Please, I want to live! She told me that she could get us close to a million for the design and research of a prototype I helped design.

She is coming in the morning with the buyer. Stacey said after the sale was done, we would leave and never be seen again."

Stacey must have been the girl in the woods. I also had a sinking feeling that she was not a random girl.

"OK, so you and Stacey are to meet here this morning. Why? You could have made the trade in the city, why out here?" Frank looked at me like I had just asked the most stupid question he ever heard.

"Why would we do the deal in the city? There are too many people around. Out here is a secret, no one knows about my cabin." He was smiling as if he said something clever.

"Frank, I knew about this place and anyone that does any background history on you, does too. How did you and Stacey meet?"

That clever smile went away and almost a realization that he was not as smart about these things as he thought. Then he told me the whole story. When he finished, I noticed the sun coming up. That only meant I would be meeting Stacey and her "buyer" soon.

There are a few things that could happen. The most likely thought was, Stacey would bring this guy to kill Frank and take what they came for. If it was me doing it, I would cut an artery and burn down the place. That way there are little to no questions.

Stacey, I was guessing, was an agent for some country that is behind on the military tech. Now, this is all me making some assumptions, but she played a long game to start a relationship with Frank and doing things with him so he would listen to her.

Frank was not a good-looking guy. He was not a skinny rail of a man or a fat guy. Frank was someone you would not notice when passing. I am also sure no one other than Stacey has called him cute in a very long time.

Stacy on the other hand, was a bit above the average-looking girl. That had to be one of the reasons she was picked. If she was too good-looking, then the mark might question things.

What I had to question was how she was going to handle things, including when she sees Frank restrained.

I thought about it a bit and put Frank in his bed all covered up. While Frank was in his bed not going anywhere, I took the external drive from his suitcase up to my car. Since it was the main reason I came, I wanted to secure it before I do anything else.

It took me a lot less time to get to my car in the morning light than I took to get to the cabin.

It was a good thing too. While I was hiding the drive, I watched a blue car fly down the road. It passes where I was parked in a little pull-off. As fast as they were going, I didn't expect them to have any working shocks for long.

I took off on foot back to the cabin. If I was lucky, I would have about five minutes before they found Frank. That would give me two minutes to prepare for whatever I needed to do.

When I got there, there was the girl from the park standing on the porch. She was with a Mediterranean guy that looked fit. He could have been a challenge to have a hand-to-hand fight with. That is why I didn't go that route. Instead, I got on the edge of the woods and aimed my gun. I was lined up on the center of his chest. After I squeezed the trigger, I shot him in the throat.

It would have been impressive if that was where I was aiming. For trying to shoot him in the chest it was bad, so I realized I needed to spend more time on the range. That would be something I would worry about another time.

Stacey turned around and saw her partner laying on the ground bleeding all over. I would have to guess that this was her real romantic interest. Stacey ran to him and held him as he was dying. As Stacey said her last goodbye to the guy, I walked up with my gun pointed at her back.

Her sobbing must have made me undetectable to her. This girl didn't think about the important questions that she should of. Instead, she put herself in harm's way.

I wonder if she was a new spy. I say spy because I don't know what those two are. Maybe she had been recruited in the same way Stacey recruited Frank. I never had time to look her up. That would explain what appeared to be a lack of training.

Mr. Stone had told me that problems are working with someone you are romantically entangled with.

Now I could see firsthand without it being me.

When I was close enough that I knew my aim was good, I spoke. "Only the dead can comfort the dead. Now get up with your hands on the back of your head and stand up."

She listened to me putting her hands on the back of her head.

As soon as she was on her feet, I lead her into the cabin. I don't know why, but I wanted to completely break Frank using the girl he had fallen in love with. I wanted to see his rage towards her. I also wanted to see if he would show rage.

Since I started working with Mr. Stone, I found myself interested in understanding people more. I had a gift before to know what people were most likely going to do before they did it. I just never understood why.

I placed her in the center of the room on her knees. After checking her for a gun and finding nothing, I went over to Frank. Lifting him up and turning him to see her, he must have forgotten everything he realized that night because seeing the tears run down her face, he began to yell at me.

"What did you do to her? I will make you pay for this!" Then he went off trying to calm Stacey. What made me laugh a little is when she snapped at him and told him the truth.

Her name was not Stacey, but Jane and her boyfriend laid on the ground outside dead.

The look on Frank's face told it all. He was broken and filled with rage. He had thrown his whole life away for a girl. A girl that he really didn't know and she had done nothing but lied to him the entire time. His entire world had crumbled on top of him.

As he was seeing things, the choices he made would leave him dead much sooner than later. Sadly, Frank was OK with this. He said "I would have done anything for you. I still love Stacey, but as for Jane, I don't care what happens to you."

That is when I started by asking who she worked for. At first, I was nice about it. By the fourth time asking, I began to smack her. It only took two more times of asking when she told me everything.

The guy on the ground was named Tolya and he was her handler. He had spent a year training her after recruiting her. She was living on the street when Tolya found her. They grew close to each other as they worked together.

Jane finally got to what I wanted to know. Tolya worked for a division in charge of recovering or obtaining information. She was meant to be a tool for that object while he was in the United States.

As for whom employed her, she didn't have a clue. He never said and she never pushed for answers. She was too grateful that he had taken her in, and she didn't want to mess things up.

Then she started to fall in love with him.

When Jane finished, I knew everything I needed to give my client a full report. Frank was still alive, and he would be taken in and I would be returning the data. I was only left to wrap everything up in a tidy little bow.

Whatever happened, I wanted to make sure that Frank knew he could not return to his life. I looked around and found that there were so many flammable things in the cabin. Plus, the cabin was made of wood.

The only question left to answer was what to do with Jane. I didn't have anything against her or any contract on her. That is why I tied her up and put her next to her dead boyfriend.

Frank wanted something more, but it didn't take much to see I didn't care what Frank wanted.

I moved Frank by the door before I went to work. I wanted Frank to know he could not come back, and this was step one. I Noticed the fire in the fireplace was nothing more than a stack of hot black and red logs.

I put the sheets of the bed on the floor and took one of the logs glowing the brightest against the pile of sheets. All it took was a couple of times blowing on the log to get the fire to go. When it did, the thin sheets started to burn, and was quickly going up in flames. Once the bed mattress started to have a nice flame coming from it, I knew I accomplished what I wanted.

Frank was screaming about all of his stuff. He had been broken by finding out the girl he loved was not the girl he knew. On top of that, she was using him. Because of her, he gave up a good job and a life he was mostly happy with. Now he watched his last connection to his life burning up.

Frank was about to face the consequences for what he did. I didn't ask what the client would do with Frank nor did I care. The only thing I cared about was how much of a pain it would be to drag Frank up to my car if he didn't go willingly.

As the flames in the cabin started to climb the walls, I cut the bindings around Frank's feet.

Expecting him to try and run, he surprised me and let me guide him out the door and stood where I placed him.

Jane, on the other hand was trying to get herself freed. She had started to cry again as she looked into the dead eyes of the man I shot. It must have been horrifying for her laying next to Tolya. On top of her being in love with the guy, his throat had a large hole covered in blood.

I even think his blood had soaked up into the ground she was laying on.

She seemed to calm down again when she noticed that I walked over to her. Before leaving with Frank, I gave her some advice. "OK, here is our deal. I don't get anything out of killing you. If you don't want me to come back to find you, you will tell the police that Frank invited you and your boyfriend out here to make nice.

When you got here, Frank lost it and shot him. He was crazy and just walked off. If you mention me or give any hint of what had really happened, I will come to find you.

If I do that, you will not die by my hands. I know a place where a group of sick guys will make you wish for death."

With nothing more to say to her, I lead Frank back to my car. He didn't say anything to me but mumbled to himself a few times. I put him in the front seat next to me. Then I explained the rules. If he does anything that I don't like, I will have to shoot him.

He told me he understood and as we drove back to Raleigh, Frank told me everything on his mind.

By the time we got into Raleigh, I knew everything Frank went through to get the data out. He explained how Stacey talked him into it and how they planned to go down to South America to live as royals would. It was a fantastic story, and I could see the romantic drive to it. I know a girl I would have done the same thing for.

Even though I could see myself doing what Frank did, I was not being paid to sympathize with him.

I was getting paid to bring the data stolen and possibly Frank back to the client. So, when I pulled into an empty parking lot, I looked around.

Wondering if I went to the wrong place, I looked over to Frank and noticed him pointing to a man. The man Frank pointed towards wore an expensive suit and a pink shirt, but no tie. He stood in front of a closed-down store. If I had to guess, it looked like it used to be a Kmart.

Not willing to risk anything, I left Frank tied up in the front seat and an external drive hidden in the back. That left me to go and see if this was the guy I came to meet with.

Walking up, I felt my gun on my backshift, but I didn't want to adjust it. The best outcome I had was that this guy walking toward me would think that at my age, I would not be trained properly. My biggest hope was he would not find me to be a threat.

Getting up close to him, I could see that he looked tired and a little distracted. This was not an ideal situation. From everything Mr. Stone taught me, people distracted at these meets tend to do or are planning to do something stupid. I was also taught to always be aware of what is going on around me.

That is why, when there was movement inside the empty store, I knew this would not go as smoothly as I hoped. I looked the man in the eyes and asked him who was inside and what he was trying to pull.

He replied quickly. "WHAT?, I mean, there is no one inside. It is just me here. Why would you think someone is inside the store?"

"You know you hired me, and I am here to provide my services and complete my end of the deal.

If you think having those guys inside plan to eliminate me, and then your guys take what I gathered for you, you will find a problem there. I will kill you and your friend, then I will take Frank with the data to someone willing to pay me. I bet they will also pay more than I am getting for this job." He looked at his shoes after I finished my little speech.

A few seconds later, he waved his hand in the air. Then a man dressed in a pair of cheap black pants and a button-up shirt came out.

This guy was hired to help and most likely was someone on a security team who had a questionable personality. I had to assume he had a gun hidden in the back of his pants too. The difference between him and me was that I had nothing covering my gun. Anyone walking behind me could easily see my gun. This guy had his button-up shirt untucked and there were no signs that the shirt was pulled up in the back.

So, I knew I would get to my gun much faster than he would. This made it easier to work with these guys. I didn't waste any more time. "Now that we are all being open here, let's take care of what we came here to do.

It will be simple; you give me my money and I give you what you want. Then we go to our own homes." I waited for them to answer and kept a smile on my face while doing so.

"You can call me Mr. Heckle. This man next to me is an employee who is here to make sure you don't try anything funny.

You can't be too safe, don't you agree?" Mr. Heckle smiled back at me and then asked us to go inside to do our business.

I will tell you that would not happen. I would not be going to where I cannot control the situation. My guess was that they had another person inside still watching. Going inside would only lead me to possibly getting myself killed.

There were a few minutes of nothing being said till I broke the silence. "Listen, Mr. Heckle, I don't know what game you're playing. Let's cut the crap and get this deal done. I am not going in there. We can make our exchange now or I can leave. What do you want to do?"

Mr. Heckle didn't say anything to me, but he whispered in the ear of his employee. His henchman went into the building and came back out with a small bag. They must not do much thinking because the guy just held out the bag. He waited for me to walk over and take it.

From past experiences, I have learned a few lessons. One of those lessons is, if you get in arms reach, then your enemy can put hands on you.

If someone can grab you, the whole situation changes, and you could lose control.

I was not going to take the chance and told the henchman to put the bag in the center of us. He did what I requested, but the guy just stood there.

I started to feel that they didn't consider me to have any intelligence.

"Hey Lurch, how about you back away? I will check the money and if all of it's there, I will give you what you have paid for." Once I made that statement, he backed away.

Once I felt it was safe to check the money, I walked up and bent down to count it. It took me three minutes to confirm that my bonus for Frank was missing. These people were starting to piss me off. I made an agreement and at every turn this shifty guy kept trying to break that agreement.

Enough is enough. I spent more time than I wanted to with these people. I went and got the drive they had paid for. It took me a little longer than I planned to get it, but I got it.

When I turned back towards this client, I saw the goon walking towards me. My first thought was that nothing good would come from this.

Instead of waiting for the guy to get within arm's reach of me, I pulled my gun. He went for his, but his shirt got in the way. You would expect most people to put their hands up.

Most people don't want to risk being shot. The henchman started to run towards me when he realized he could not get his gun.

The somewhat quiet community got very noisy when I squeezed off three rounds. One missed, but two of them got Mr. Running Bull in the hip and dropped him. Now the clock was running. From what I was told, it is safe to assume police would show up within three minutes of a gunshot.

With one guy down, another came running out of the building to help. I pulled my gun up towards him and he did stop and put his hands up.

Since no one was moving now, I quickly walked over to Mr. Heckle and handed him the drive.

Backing up as quickly as I could, I grabbed my money and left with Frank. I pulled out of the parking lot and passed about three cop cars flying down the road. I was hoping Mr. Heckle would be smart enough not to mention me if he got caught. Giving my information up would not end well for him and his bosses.

I didn't wait and got out of town. It looked as I had a travel mate for the next few hours. Personally, I thought it would be rude to keep him tied up. I stopped for gas when we got to what I felt was a safe distance from Raleigh that we would not be followed.

Once I untied Frank, he gave me a now what look. To be honest, I didn't plan for Frank to come with me. If I knew things would have turned out the way they did, I would have left Frank with his fake girlfriend. Instead, he had now become my responsibility.

I offered Frank what I thought was a good deal. Before we left the gas station, I told him he could get out there and do whatever he wanted.

The other option I gave him was to ride with me to Washington DC. From there, he could hide in the city or hop on a train somewhere else.

He didn't take long to think about it, and he decided to ride with me to Washington DC. For the next three and half hours, we watched the road that led us to the future.

For me, it would be my next job. For Frank, it would be a new life and a new name. I could feel for him since I had recently gone through that myself.

It was mostly quiet as I drove. The radio played, but we didn't say much. I didn't want to talk too much and give away anything about myself. Frank, I imagine was trying to figure out what he would do. All of his plans had fallen through, and he lost everything for a girl that played him.

When I pulled up to Union Station in DC. Frank went to get out but stopped. "Why did you not just kill me and instead help me get away? I don't think you feel sorry for me." With that said, Frank looked down and sighed.

"OK, Frank, let me explain this to you. I got hired to retrieve the stolen data. I would get a bonus to turn you over with the data. Luckily for you, they didn't pay the bonus. I am not one to give away something for nothing. Now they have a world of trouble, and you have the chance to start over. I would make the most of it if I was you."

He smiled at this and thanked me. Watching him walk towards the train station was the last I saw or heard of Frank.

With my first solo job done, I went home to call Mr. Stone and see what was next.

E.A. Maynard

Chapter Seven

Tales of a drunk assassin

IT WAS A COLD WINTER evening and I had gone to Baltimore, Maryland for some business. There is nothing exciting about what I do. I design custom high-end restaurants and bars. Outside of my field, no one would know my name. The clients sometimes had problems remembering my name, although I don't know what is so hard to remember.

Who can't remember Kane? I mean, it's one of the oldest names in the world. The client I was seeing was just as bad with calling me Cam. So, it was not hard to turn down his offer to join him for drinks. I used the same excuses I had with all the other clients.

I simply told him that I made it company policy that no one is allowed to drink with clients or vendors. Most understood and let it go after that, but then there were people like the guy in Baltimore. He asked, "You are the owner of your firm, so you can break your own rules and who would know?" People like him are the same people that believe they are above all rules.

He had money and knew people of power in his town. He played to their vices and his own. These are the same people that caused me to make the rule. I had a feeling that he would try to get me to say or do something he could hold over me. This made it easier for me to decline his offer again.

After wrapping up with some issues I needed to confirm with him, it was time for me to do my homework. I had found out the two most popular restaurants and two bars in the area. I found out that Baltimore was very much in love with their crabs and oysters. The first restaurant I went to, had an impressive design.

The kitchen jetted out into the dining room with glass walls splitting them apart. It gave the feel that you were able to be in the kitchen with the staff. The equipment shined as if it was being used for the first time. All I could think about was the amount of work that went into cleaning it. The food was good, but I liked the entertainment the diners got from watching the staff move around and make the food.

Finishing my dinner, I asked my waiter about where to go for a good drink at the same level of the restaurant. At first, I thought he would suggest the restaurant bar, but instead he suggested a bar his buddy was working at. It was a hidden bar in an area called Fells Point. From what the waiter told me, the bar was not known by the police in general or most people. Rather, it is where the upper class of people could be found.

My interest was piqued and I got directions. When the waiter came back with my bill, he also had instructions on entering the bar. The bar was able to be accessed through a bookstore. It was not as simple as walking through a door. Instead, I first had to ask for a book by the name of Country Secrets. After the store owner tells me they are sold out, I was to say it was OK since I read it already.

The store owner then directed me to go back through the stock room. I noticed only two doors back there. One led me out to the alley in the back and the other looked like a closet, although it was not. That door led to the building next to the bookstore.

A middle-aged guy sat at the door looking as if he was on the verge of going to sleep. When I reached out to grab the door handle, the guy spoke up. "I don't know you and I don't like people I don't know. So why don't you tell me who you are."

He looked up at me and pushed back his jacket to show he had a gun handy. So that told me that I was in the right place and security is something they take seriously. Those two reasons are why I didn't hesitate to say my name is Kane and I was sent by James the waiter.

The middle—aged guy with the gun look down at his smartphone. After about thirty seconds of him sliding through the screen, he stopped and looked up at me and nodded, giving me permission to enter. The bar put me in mind of what I would expect an old 1920's speak easy would look like. The walls were a red painted brick and had wood benches with tables towards the back. The front had sofas and chairs with side tables. The bar had no chairs to sit and it didn't look like people went to the bar.

Looking around, I found a chair that was mostly private. It allowed me to see the entire place while not bothering anyone. When I went to sit down, a waiter came up asking for my order. Letting myself sink into the chair, I ordered an Old Fashion. The waiter smiled and said "Yes sir, may I suggest the houses version of the old fashion? The bartender is very proud of it and others find it enjoyable."

As I went to answer, a guy in his fifties spoke up. "Give it to him, if he does not like it, I will take it and buy him the traditional version." Nothing more needed said and the waiter was gone.

Looking at his grey hair, green eyes, and custom-tailored clothes, I thanked him and introduced myself. He introduced himself as Charles Stone in a soothing voice. He didn't appear to be someone from old money or someone who thought of himself as if he were above others. We both were in a private bar hidden away from the rest of the world.

After a while of talking and a few drinks, I asked what he did for a living. The look on his face was odd from such a simple question. Charles began to look around and looked at me. Rather than answer, he redirected the question to what I do. I explained how my company designs restaurant and bars for the high-end businesses. I didn't think it was very interesting, but Charles asked all sorts of questions and seemed very interested.

This went on for at least one more drink when he told me he was a fixer. I had heard of fixers before, and what I knew of them, they would do illegal things to make problems for the elite go away. My thought would be something along the lines of bribing people and paying off people to go away. Perhaps like the rich man's son got a girl knocked up, so he would give her some money and suggest a nice town three states away to start over.

I made a few jokes about him fixing my issues with my client and the local building inspector. As I said, I was joking, but he pulled out his phone and made a call. "Hello Tom. You know who this is. I still noticed you going to Phillip's house. I imagine your wife and kids still don't know that, though. I also imagine the restaurant a new friend of mine named Kane is working on, will have an easier time going through your office." Charles sat there for a few moments and thanked the guy before hanging up.

Charles smiled and said, "It looks like he knew you, so that is good for two reasons. Now I know you are who you say you are, and you now have one less problem to worry about." I could only blink and make sure my mouth was not open.

"What just happened? Did you call the inspector and black mail him?" The response I got from my questions was simply indicating the deputy mayor hated his phone calls. Either way, the subject was changed back to him and his line of work. I could see the drinks starting to have a real effect on him.

Charles Looked at me as he was relaxing in his seat and said he wanted to tell me a story. It was something he had not told anyone other than his client. It had not been spoken about for a decade or more. He felt now was the right time to tell this story.

Honestly, I figured he was drunk when he started the tale. He ordered us another round and got himself more comfortable in his chair. His eyes locked on mine and without any effort, his eyes looked void of any joy. I would say that the thoughts going through his mind must have been hidden in a dark place.

When our drinks came and the waiter walked away, he began his story. Charles voice was cold and sounded like a different man talking. The joyful man had vanished and was replaced with a guy who put a chill in me. I even remember that the first sentence he said gave me goose bumps.

"I had to kill a congressman, said Charles. He was having an affair with a sixteen-year-old girl and from what I was told, he had crossed too many lines. With all of his illegal and questionable activity, if one article came out, then the other stuff he was doing would follow. The problem was that several other politicians would be discovered at the same time in what would be considered treasonous acts."

Charles continued. "I followed the Congressman for two weeks and watched everything he was doing. Let's say I had no issues with killing him after that.

One night, I followed him and the teenager to a hotel in Bethesda Maryland. It took me some work, some promises, and a hundred dollars to get the room number. Before I left the guy at the front desk, I informed him that it would be best for his health to forget I was there.

When I got up to the floor he was on, there was a young couple making out at the end of the hallway and another guy was passed out drunk sleeping in his doorway. The door was held open by his hip. I dragged the guy into his room and found a bottle of Jack Daniels almost empty sitting on the standby the TV.

That is when it came to me. I took a drink of the whiskey and took the guys shirt he was wearing. The drunk had to be sweating everything he had drank and his shirt soaked it all up. With the guys shirt on and my breath smelling of liquor, I went to the Congressman's room.

Aftermath (Bearman Series)

Once I was at the door, I tried to use the drunk's key card to get into the room. When it didn't work like I knew it wouldn't, I started to knock on the door and asked for a Lisa to let me in. After a few failed attempts, he must have got tired of the noise. When the door started to open, I pushed my way into the room. The Congressman fell back, and the young girl covered herself.

I moved quickly, pulled my knife and cut his femoral and radial arteries. While he bled out, I began to punch him so that it would look as though he was attacked in a violent rage. Then with him inches from death, I stabbed him five more times. The mission was complete and I was about to leave until I heard a whimper. It was the girl, and she knew what I looked like.

With her in tears, I sat down in a chair that was across from the bed. I wanted to think about what I could do to make it easier on her. While I sat there, she started to tell me about how she didn't have a choice. Her Parents rented her to men for five hundred a night and it had been going on for two years.

It was hard but she told me who handled the exchange and set up everything. I knew that she couldn't help me with anything from that point. She knew what I looked like and if I let her go, she would be back to her family being sold off at a nightly rate.

So, I put my hands over her nose and mouth to cut off her ability to breath. She didn't fight me, but almost felt as she welcomed it. I expected her to grab my hands and try to push them away. Instead, she grabbed the sheets and closed her eyes. Then just before she died, her eyes opened.

In all my life, I had done some terrible things. I have never felt bad about anything I did. That was except for killing that young girl. I still see the look on her face and wonder what she thought in her final moments.

I took the Congressman's stuff and left a single dollar bill with the back side facing up. The people who contracted me didn't tell me why they wanted a dollar left on him and why the back had to face up. I simply asked how much I would be getting paid.

Years later, I found out more than I should about the group that hired me. Now, after all these years and all the work I had done for them, they turned on me."

Charles sat there not saying another word. He took a drink and staired past me. Normally I would have not believed a word that was said, but this guy had me convinced. People don't have the look that this guy had on his face without being honest.

Finally, I had to break the silence and ask him questions. How could I not? The first thing I wanted to know was why he was telling me. I mean, why tell a stranger in a bar about a crime that could send him to prison for life.

When I asked him, he seemed to break out of his trance and look at me again. Charles calmly smiled and told me. "When I said they turned on me, I mean they put a hit on me. I had killed a good number of people for this group. My first contact had become a President of the United States of America and I guess I am a loose end. My friend called me and told me that he got a call to do the job."

I could not help myself. "What kind of friends do you have? They will call you and tell you that they are going to kill you. Who does that? Why would he do that?" I would have gone on, but Charles put his hand up to tell me to wait. Then signaled the waiter for another round.

The buzz I had slipped away and I sat on the edge of my seat. I was talking to a hit man. Not one of those guys who you know is a criminal and pay them for something they never done before. This was the kind of hitman that movies are based off of. The kind of stories authors are writing about.

Once the waiter dropped off another round, he told me. "My friend is a guy I trained years ago. A guy who went freelance, but sometimes take a job he doesn't want. This would be one of those jobs. He took it so I could choose how I go out. I am not going to let someone sneak up and kill me in an alley or smother me in my sleep. Instead, I am going to go out like the gentleman I am.

My friend will be waiting for me once I leave here. I would imagine he is parked outside now waiting to give me a ride home. From there, he will end it. I will go out like a man and he will be the one who gets paid for it. That is what I want and that is why he is doing it."

I didn't know what to say. What do you say? I wanted to see him tell me he was joking or pulling my leg. It could not be real, after all. I had to know, so I asked questions about his past and about his life, thinking he would say something to tell me how false his story was. That was not the case.

He left after finishing his drink and put five hundred dollars on the table. As he walked away, he told me that the money should cover the bill, and I just need to leave the tip. That was the last thing I heard from Charles Stone. He walked out as if he only had a single drink.

I was feeling buzzed, but with the adrenaline rushing through my veins, I was nowhere as drunk as I should have been. The rest of my stay in Baltimore was quiet and profitable. I used a few ideas I picked up in later designs.

Many things were going through my head about the project I was working on, and the other project I would need to start. When I got to the airport and through TSA, I saw a news stand. I bought a local paper and went to my gate.

Once I was all settled in, I read the paper while waiting. The paper had some good writing, and you could see the love for the Baltimore Ravens the writer had. I got to the entertainment section and it was unimpressive, but OK writing. I was about to put the paper aside when I saw a headline that I could not miss.

The article was about a man who was murdered in his home. The man murdered was sitting in his chair when found. He was shot at point blank range in the heart. The gun was found next to the chair along with a dollar bill back facing up.

It talked about how there was not much known about Charles Stone. He was a 68-year-old consultant. The police are looking for leads and asking anyone with information to come forward. After that, I don't know what was written. I dropped the paper on the ground and stared off to nothing.

I pulled myself together and got on my flight for home. From the story I was told, I knew it was best if I didn't say a word to any police. So, now Mr. Stone's story will be just that, a story told. Whatever you want to think, I will remember the night I was told a sobering story from a drunk assassin.